"I miss you, Savannah."

God, Charlie hated making that admission, but the words had jumped from him.

"Then don't go," she whispered. "Stay with me and let's make this right."

His heart squeezed in his chest so tightly he thought it might pop. Part of him longed to take her into his arms and promise her anything she wanted, just so long as she'd keep touching him. But there were too many reasons for him to go for him to do that. He could never be what she needed him to be.

"I can't do that."

"Why not?"

Her eyes locked with his, she moved closer, her body so near he could feel her heat.

"Why can't you just change your mind and stay with me?"

"It's not that simple." He swallowed. Hard.

"It's as simple as you make it." Her gaze darted to the movement at his throat, then she fully pressed herself against him, her lips grazing against his neck.

He closed his eyes, knowing he was about to give in to the very real need within him. His lips covered hers and his body sighed with relief, with recognition of the woman kissing him. He had missed her. So very much.

Her taste. Her smell. The feel of her. Everything.

"I want you so much, Savannah."

Dear Reader,

I instantly connected with Nurse Savannah Carter, and found myself going through many of the same emotions as she did while dealing with sexy but frustrating Dr Charlie Keele.

Charlie is a bit of a rambling man. He thinks he's no good for Savannah—or any woman—and he usually doesn't allow himself to get attached. Unfortunately he is second-guessing the career opportunity of a lifetime because of his relationship with Savannah. Which means he has to take it.

Savannah was raised to be a strong, independent woman, and she's quite proud of those traits. So when Charlie breaks things off not only is her heart broken, her pride is severely wounded. And now there's a baby on the way.

Together they have to overcome the past, deal with the present and forge a future. I hope you enjoy their story as much as I did. I love to hear from readers, so feel free to shoot me an email at janice@janicelynn.net.

Happy reading,

Janice

THE NURSE'S
BABY SECRET

BY
JANICE LYNN

MILLS & BOON

First published in Great Britain 2017
By Mills & Boon, an imprint of HarperCollins*Publishers*
1 London Bridge Street, London, SE1 9GF

Large Print edition 2017

© 2017 Janice Lynn

ISBN: 978-0-263-06728-6

Printed and bound in Great Britain
by CPI Antony Rowe, Chippenham, Wiltshire

Janice Lynn has a master's in nursing from Vanderbilt University, and works as a nurse practitioner in a family practice. She lives in the southern United States with her husband, their four children, their Jack Russell—appropriately named Trouble—and a lot of unnamed dust bunnies that have moved in since she started her writing career. To find out more about Janice and her writing visit janicelynn.com.

Books by Janice Lynn

Mills & Boon Medical Romance

After the Christmas Party...
Flirting with the Doc of Her Dreams
New York Doc to Blushing Bride
Winter Wedding in Vegas
Sizzling Nights with Dr Off-Limits
It Started at Christmas...

Visit the Author Profile page
at millsandboon.co.uk for more titles.

**Janice won
The National Readers' Choice Award
for her first book
*The Doctor's Pregnancy Bombshell***

To Jessie & Rebecca—
may your love story be one for the ages.

CHAPTER ONE

NURSE SAVANNAH CARTER stared at her flat lower abdomen via the reflection in her bedroom mirror, imagining she saw the tiniest outline of a bulge if she stood just right.

Pregnant. Her.

How long had she dreamed of this moment?

Years. Her whole life.

She'd always wanted children. Always.

Sure, she'd thought she'd be married and have a husband who was going to be an amazing father to her precious child, but since when had things gone according to plan?

Never, really. Just as this pregnancy wasn't planned. But she couldn't complain. She had a good life. A great life. A great man in her life.

Charlie Keele was a wonderful person and doctor, and if her baby ended up with a more than generous share of Charlie's genetic code, well, her baby would be a blessed child.

Charlie was brilliant, gorgeous, athletic, a man

who respected her independence and beliefs, and he'd been Lucky Savannah's boyfriend for the past year.

Lucky Savannah. She smiled at the nickname. That was what her friends had been calling her since the first time Charlie had singled her out at the hospital. They'd teased even more as she and Charlie had slid into an exclusive relationship. These days she and Charlie were inseparable. They exercised together, ate more meals together than not, worked together, and practically lived together. She suspected they would soon. For quite some time she'd been expecting Charlie to ask her to move in with him.

Expecting him to propose.

Charlie owned a beautiful brick home with lots of room and an amazing fenced-in backyard just right for a family, in an up-and-coming neighborhood. If he hadn't mentioned living together first, when her apartment lease came up for renewing, she planned to discuss moving in with him.

She was having Charlie's baby. That might rush things a bit, which she regretted. She wanted him to ask her to live with him, to marry him, when he was ready, because he couldn't imagine spending the rest of his life without her. She had no doubt that was where their relationship was headed and she had no regrets regarding her accidental pregnancy.

She wanted Charlie and she wanted his baby.

Although she'd dated in the past, she'd never met a man like Charlie. Never felt for a man what she felt for Charlie. Never felt as cherished as Charlie made her feel. It was what her parents had had prior to her father's death when Savannah was seven years old. It was what Savannah had always known she'd hold out for. She didn't need a man, but having a good one in her life gave a shiny glow to everything.

A shiny glow she'd found with Charlie.

She pressed her hand over her belly, trying to imagine that she could feel the little life inside her. Charlie's baby.

Her and Charlie's baby.

A miniature version of them growing inside her.

Savannah's smile widened as her imagination took off. His brown hair and eyes and her fair skin? Or his strong, handsome facial features and cleft chin and her blue eyes? Or maybe her red hair and his dark features? Or…the possibilities were endless. Regardless, their baby would be beautiful. Would be loved. Would be their whole world.

A baby!

They'd not talked about children, but Charlie would be happy. He loved her. He hadn't said the words out loud, but Savannah knew. She saw it in the way he looked at her, in the way he touched her, kissed her, treated her as if she was the center of his world. Charlie Keele was in love with her and would be ecstatic at their news.

She really was a lucky woman.

She was having the most wonderful man in the world's baby. They were going to be a family and have a fabulous life.

Feeling as if she was floating, she glanced at her watch. He'd be here in a couple of hours. She'd tell him their news. He'd kiss her, twirl her around, sweep her off her feet, maybe even propose. Something grand, for sure.

Her hair and make-up were done up a little more than her usual ponytail pullback and light coating of mascara, just in case.

Maybe she should drop some hints and let him figure out her news in some creative way. Like a blue and pink cupcake or maybe she could get him to take her to a toy store under the guise of picking up a gift for her friend Chrissie's son, Joss. They could stroll through the baby section and she could ooh and aah over the tiny little outfits. Or she could fill up his car with pink and blue balloons or... A dozen reveal ideas came to her, each one putting a bigger smile on her face.

Wouldn't he be surprised when he realized?

Reality was, she'd never be able to keep the news from him for long. Already she was about to pop with excitement just waiting for him to arrive. No doubt he'd take one look at her and know.

She probably had a pregnancy glow.

Savannah laughed out loud, the happy sound echoing around her bathroom.

They were having a baby.

A baby! How amazing was that?

Needing to burn some of her energy while she waited for him, she hid the pregnancy test she'd done when her menstrual cycle had failed to make an appearance. Even if he beat her back, she wanted to see his face when he found out he was going to be a father.

When all evidence was safely tucked away, she grabbed her purse to head to the nearest department store.

There were some little pink and blue items she just had to have.

* * *

Frowning, Dr. Charlie Keele stared at the contract on his desk.

The signed and countersigned contract.

He'd done it.

He'd debated back and forth over the past month, but he'd really done it. He'd signed on to accept a job two hours away.

Taking the position was an amazing opportunity, but he had hesitated and he'd known why.

Savannah.

She'd become such an intrinsic part of his life, completely entangled in everything he did. He struggled to imagine leaving Chattanooga and the most remarkable woman he'd ever known.

But every time he'd considered turning down the offer, the past had reared its ugly head, reminding him of all the reasons why he should go.

He'd signed his name on that line for Savannah as much as for himself. More.

Savannah was an incredible woman. One unlike any he'd ever known or dated. Sure, he'd had a few long-term relationships over the years, but none that he'd ever thought twice about walking away from. Walking away had always been easy.

Nothing about leaving Chattanooga would be

easy, except knowing that he was doing the right thing for Savannah by leaving before she became any more attached.

She was the most independent woman he'd ever met. He'd not expected her to get so intertwined in his life. Nor had he expected himself to become so tangled up in hers.

"Don't let a woman hold you back from your dream, son."

How many times had he heard that or something similar over the years? His father had dreamt of medical school, of working as a travel doctor with an organization such as Doctors Without Borders, of dedicating his life to medicine. Instead, he'd gotten his girlfriend pregnant, dropped out of college and gotten a coal-mining job to support his new family.

He'd resented his wife and child every day since for those stolen dreams. Charlie's mother and Charlie had never been able to replace those dreams and his father had grown more and more bitter over the years. Rupert Keele had pushed Charlie toward going into the medical profession from the time Charlie could walk and talk. Talking about medicine, about becoming a doctor and traveling the world to take care of needy people, was the one time Charlie's father liked having him around. For years Charlie had thought if he could make his father proud, that might make his father love him, might make life better for himself and his mother. He'd tried his best but, no matter how good the grade, the game performance, the above and beyond achievement, nothing had ever been good enough. Rupert hadn't cared one iota about anything or anyone except himself.

Charlie's mother hadn't been much better, blaming Charlie for her lot in life as well.

Sometimes Charlie wondered if he'd have chosen something besides medicine if he hadn't been brainwashed from birth and so eager to try to win his mostly uninterested father's affections in the hopes it would somehow magically transform his parents into good ones. Regardless, when Charlie had been eleven, his maternal grandfather's congestive heart failure had worsened and Charlie had decided that, rather than work as a travel doctor, he wanted to do cardiology, to work on healing people's physical hearts, because he sure hadn't been able to do anything with his parents'.

Charlie had dreamed of heading up a cardiology unit his whole life and now he had the chance.

* * *

If he'd learned nothing else from his parents, he'd learned giving up one's dreams only led to misery for all concerned and that he couldn't protect anyone from that misery, not himself or the people he cared about.

Which was why he was leaving Chattanooga to set Savannah free.

To truly accomplish that, he'd have to hurt her, make her hate him.

Based on past experience, that should be no problem.

Stuffing the last of the shopping bags into her closet, Savannah closed the door just as her doorbell rang.

Charlie was there.

Finally.

He had a key but always rang the bell rather than just coming in, as she'd asked him time and again.

She turned from the closet and a pair of blue baby booties sitting on the bed caught her eye.

Oops.

She grabbed up the soft cotton booties, hugged them to her for one brief happy moment, then put them in the closet with her other purchases and re-closed the door. She'd decided she was just going to place his hand on her belly and let him figure out for himself why. She'd watch as his face lit with surprise, then excitement. She felt so giddy her insides quivered.

"You okay?" Charlie asked when she opened her apartment door, his dark eyes curious as she had taken longer than usual.

By way of an answer, she wrapped her arms around his neck and pressed her lips to his.

Immediately, his arms went around her waist and pulled her close, kissing her back. A thousand butterflies took flight in her belly that had nothing to do with the little life growing there and everything to do with the man making her heart race.

His kisses always made her heart race.

"Hmm," he mused, looking confused, when he pulled back from her mouth. "What was that for?"

"Do I have to have a reason to kiss you?" she asked, batting her lashes. She wanted to just tell him, to jump up and down and scream to the world that she was having a baby—Charlie's baby. But, seriously, she should probably let him into the apartment and close the front door before doing so.

Probably.

Frowning, he shook his head. "You have to admit, that's not the usual way you greet me."

"Well, it should be." He was right. She didn't meet him at the door and throw herself at him usually, but nothing was usual about tonight. Tonight, she was going to tell him the greatest news.

His brow lifted in question.

About to burst with excitement, she searched for the right words. Loving the strong feel of him, the spicy smell of him she wanted to breathe in until he permeated all her senses. "I have good news."

She was about bursting to tell him. But it registered that he'd yet to smile, as his face took on a tired appearance and he closed his eyes, tension tightening his body. "I have something to tell you, too."

"You do?" She stepped back and motioned for him to come into her apartment. Rather than sitting down, he paced across to the opposite side of the living room.

"Yes, and maybe I should go first." He raked his fingers through his hair, turned, gave her a troubled look.

The cloud nine Savannah had been walking on all afternoon dissipated and she felt her stomach drop. She'd been off work, but had met him that morning to run at the greenway. Then, they'd hit the gym together for about an hour. He'd been all smiles when he'd walked her to her car and kissed her goodbye. He'd kissed her so thoroughly and soundly that she'd wanted to drag him into the backseat and have her way with him.

Not that that was anything new. She always wanted to have her way with Charlie. He had *that* kind of body. One she still had difficulty believing she got to see and touch and kiss and hold and...

She shook off the sensual rabbit hole her mind was jumping down. "What's going on?"

"I didn't mean to get into this first thing." He paced over to a bookshelf, picked up a framed photo of them at Lookout Mountain, stared at the smiling image of them as if he'd never seen it before rather than being part of the couple in the picture. "But it's just as well to get it out in the open."

He was the most upfront person she knew. She'd never seen him so distracted. Was something wrong?

"Charlie?"

He set the photo down, turned and faced her. His expression was clouded, which was odd. Charlie never tried to keep his feelings from her. He'd never had to. He knew she was as crazy about him as he was about her.

Only right now, at this moment, he didn't look like a man who was crazy about her. He looked like a man who was torn by whatever he was about to say, a man who was about to deliver earth-shattering news.

Fear seized Savannah's heart and she struggled to get enough oxygen into her constricted lungs.

"Charlie?" she repeated, this time with more urgency.

"Have a seat, Savannah."

She made her way to her sofa. Slowly, she sat down and waited for him to tell her what was going on. She didn't like his odd behavior, didn't like that he hadn't greeted her with smiles the way he generally did, didn't like the way her heart worked overtime.

Where was her loving, kind, generous, open lover of the past year? The man whose entire face would light with happiness when he saw her? The man whose eyes would eat her up with possessiveness and desire and magical feel-good vibes?

The man avoiding looking directly at her looked as if he was about to deliver the news that she had a terminal illness or something just as devastating.

What if…? Her hands trembled.

Oh, God. Please don't let something be wrong with Charlie. Please, no.

Not now. Not ever.

"I'm leaving."

His two simple words echoed around the room, not registering in Savannah's mind.

"What?" Her chest muscles contracted tightly around her ribcage as she tried to process what he was saying, her brain still going to something possibly being wrong with him. "What do you mean that you're leaving?"

His expression guarded, he shrugged. "I'm leaving Chattanooga. I've taken a cardiology position at Vanderbilt Medical Center in Nashville on the heart failure team and I'm moving there as soon as I can get everything arranged. I turned my notice in at the hospital today."

Her ears roared. What he was saying didn't make sense. "You're leaving the hospital?"

He nodded. "I'm working out a two months' notice, during which time I'll be relocating to Nashville."

"But…your house." The house she'd imagined them raising their child in. The big backyard. The nice neighborhood close to good schools. The large rooms. Perfect for a family.

"I'll put it up for sale. I only bought it because I knew I could turn it for a profit. I never meant to stay there. It's way too big for my needs."

Never meant to stay. Too big for his needs. Savannah's head spun.

He'd never meant to stay.

Nothing he said made sense. Not to her way of thinking. Not to the promises she'd seen in his eyes, felt in his touch.

"You've always known you'd leave Chattanooga?"

She liked Chattanooga. The mountains. The river. The nightlife. The people. The town. She liked it. Chattanooga was home, where she wanted to be.

"I've never stayed in one place more than a few years and even once I'm in Nashville, if the opportunity comes along to further my career elsewhere, I'll move."

Her brain didn't seem to be processing anything correctly. Perhaps it was baby brain. Perhaps it was that he'd dropped the bottom out of her world.

"This is about your career?" she asked slowly,

trying to make sure she understood what he was saying.

Because she didn't understand anything he was saying.

He was happy in Chattanooga. Why would he willingly leave? Why hadn't she known he planned to leave some day?

"I've taken a teaching and research position at the university and a prestigious position at the hospital. It's a great opportunity."

What he said registered. Sort of. "You're moving to Nashville?"

He nodded. "The hospital is offering a relocation package. Hopefully, I'll find something to buy or rent within the next few weeks so I can be settled in prior to starting."

"Hopefully," she mumbled a little sarcastically.

He was leaving. Not once had he said a word to her about the possibility that he might leave. Not once had he mentioned that he was looking for another job. That he'd consider another job even if it was handed to him on a silver platter.

He'd made the decision without even discussing it with her. Her mother, family, and friends were here. She didn't want to move to Nashville. Upset didn't begin to cover it.

"I don't want to live two hours away from the man I'm dating," she pointed out what she thought should be obvious. "I like that I see you every morning, that we work out together, that I get to see you from time to time at work, that I get to grab dinner with you, that you get to kiss me good-night almost every single night." Did she sound whiny? If so, too bad. She felt whiny. And angry. How could he take a job in Nashville? "That's not going to happen if you're in Nashville and I'm in Chattanooga. Do you expect me to just sit around waiting for you to have time to come home or that I'm going to be commuting back and forth to Nashville between shifts?"

He regarded her for long moments, his expression guarded. "I don't expect you to do either."

What he was saying hit her.

A knife twisted in her heart and she instantly rejected the idea.

That couldn't be what he meant.

Of course that was what he was saying. That he'd not even mentioned he was thinking about moving, about taking a different job, that she hadn't warranted that tidbit of information, spoke volumes. *He was breaking up with her.*

"You've never mentioned that you planned to

move." Her words sounded lame even to herself. So what? She was reeling.

Reeling.

Maybe he meant for her to go with him. Maybe he wasn't ending things. Maybe she'd jumped to all the wrong conclusions when he'd said he was leaving. Maybe he looked so stressed because he was worried she wouldn't go with him.

The reality was she didn't want to move to Nashville. She loved her job and coworkers at Chattanooga Memorial Hospital. She wanted to stay in her hometown, to be near her family, her friends, all the things that were familiar. She wanted to raise her baby near her home, where her child would grow up knowing her family and being surrounded by their love.

Her baby.

She was pregnant.

Charlie was leaving.

With obvious annoyance, he crossed his arms. "I never mentioned that I planned to stay, either."

Ouch. Had she seen blood oozing from her chest, she wouldn't have been surprised. His comment wounded that much.

"No," she began, wondering how she could have been so terribly wrong about his feelings.

His eyes were narrowed, his tone almost accusing. "Nor have I ever implied that I would stay."

He was right. He hadn't. She'd been the one to make assumptions. Very wrong assumptions.

Her silence must have gotten to him because he paced across the room, then turned to her with a reproving look.

"Good grief, Savannah. I've taken a job that's a wonderful opportunity. Be happy for me."

Tears burned her eyes, but she refused to let them fall. Instead of telling him what he wanted to hear, she shook her head. "No, I'm not going to say I'm happy for you. Not when this news came about the way it did. We've been involved for months. You should have told me you planned to move. I deserved a warning about something so big. For that matter, we should have discussed this before you made that decision."

His jaw worked back and forth. "I don't have to have your permission to move or take a different job, Savannah."

If she weren't sitting on the sofa, she'd likely have staggered back from his verbal blow. Truly, there must be a gaping hole in her chest because her very heart had been yanked from her body. "Agreed. You don't."

"I never meant for you to think I'd stay in Chattanooga, or that I wanted to stay."

She interpreted that as he'd never meant for her to assume he was going to stay, or want to stay, with her.

She'd been such a fool. She'd believed he loved her, had believed the light in his eyes when he looked at her was love, the real deal. She'd just seen what she'd wanted to see. Whatever that look had been, she'd never seen or felt it with past boyfriends. Maybe she'd mistaken phenomenal sexual chemistry with love. She wouldn't be the first woman to have done so in the history of the world.

Devastation and anger competed for priority in her betrayed head.

She met his gaze and refused to look away, despite how much staring into his dark eyes hurt. They were ending. She'd thought everything had been so perfect and he'd been planning their end. "I think you should leave," she began, knowing that she wasn't going to be able to hold her grief in much longer and not wanting him to witness her emotional breakdown.

She was going to break down. Majorly.

He started to say something but, shoulders straight, chin tilted upward, she stopped him.

"That you made this decision without involving me tells me everything I need to know about our relationship, Charlie. We aren't on the same page and apparently never were. My bad. Now that I know we don't want the same things from our relationship, there is no relationship. I want you to leave. We're through."

There. She'd been the first one to say the words out loud. Sure, he'd been dancing all around the truth of it, but she'd put them out there.

Not once since she'd seen that little blue line appear had she considered that he wouldn't be happy about the news…that he wouldn't be there for their child.

That he wouldn't be there, period.

CHAPTER TWO

CHARLIE SMILED AT the petite lady he'd grown quite fond of over the past couple of years he'd been her cardiologist. "Now, now, Mrs. Evans. You'll be just fine under Dr. Flowers' care. He's an excellent cardiologist."

"But you know me," the woman explained, not happy about his announcement that he was relocating. "If it wasn't for having to cross that mountain halfway in between, I'd follow you to Nashville."

"I'm flattered that you'd even consider doing so, but you don't need a cardiologist who is two hours away. Mountain or no mountain, that's not a good plan."

"Then I guess you should change your mind and stay."

If ever there was a time he considered changing his mind about his move it would have been the night before at Savannah's apartment. The betrayed look on her face had gutted him, but he'd accomplished what he'd set out to do.

He'd set Savannah free and let her keep her pride by her being the one to say the words. He'd needed to let her out, but he hadn't wanted to break her spirit.

Things were as they should be.

He was single, free to make the decisions for his life without her or any woman's interference, and she was free of him and his baggage.

His father's dying words had been pleas to Charlie never to be controlled by what was in his pants, and a declaration that no woman was worth giving up one's dreams.

"Marriage and kids suck the life right out of you, son," his father had told him. "You go after your dreams and you make them happen. You be the best doctor this country has ever seen and don't you let a woman stand in your way, no matter how pretty she is. In the long run, she will eat at your soul until you despise her for taking away your dreams."

Those had been the exact words from his last conversation with his father. He'd heard similar all his life, had known that was how his father felt about his mother, him.

Although he'd become way too involved with Savannah for far too long, Charlie wouldn't let any woman tie him down.

Not because of his father, but because of not wanting to relive the hell of what he'd grown up with. He'd been a burden to his parents, had ruined their lives; he'd been unable to protect his mother from his father's abuse, unable to protect her from the misery he'd caused. Charlie would never marry nor have children. Never.

He'd ruined enough lives during his lifetime already.

"You hear something different, doc?"

Charlie blinked at the elderly woman he'd been checking and instantly felt remorse at his mental slip into the past. Crazy that this move had him thinking so much about his parents, his failure of a family, his past. All things he did his best to keep buried. Maybe that had been the problem over the past year. He'd kept his past so deeply buried that he'd forgotten all the reasons why he shouldn't have gotten so involved with Savannah. No more.

"No," he told the woman with a forced smile. "Just listening to your heart sounds. Your heart is in rhythm today."

"My heart is in rhythm every day. Just some days that rhythm isn't such a good one."

He finished examining her, then saw the rest of his morning patients. Typically, this was the time he'd go to the cardiovascular intensive care unit, see his inpatients, see if his favorite CVICU nurse could sneak away to grab a bite of lunch.

He'd gotten too attached to Savannah.

For both their sakes, he'd been right to take the job in Nashville. She might not realize it yet, but he'd done her the greatest favor of her life.

"You don't seem yourself today."

Savannah glanced up at her nurse supervisor, who also happened to be one of her dearest friends. Should she tell Chrissie the truth?

If so, how much of the truth?

The man I thought I was spending the rest of my life with told me last night that he's moving two hours away? Or, *I'm pregnant by a man I was crazy about but currently just want to strangle?*

Neither seemed the right thing to say at work, where she had to hold it together and not cry out her frustrations.

"I'm okay."

Chrissie's brow lifted. "You usually walk around

as if your feet aren't affected by gravity. I've not seen you smile all day. So I'm not buying 'okay'."

Savannah gave a semblance of a smile that was mostly bared teeth.

Chrissie winced. "That bad?"

Savannah nodded. "Worse."

"You and Charlie have an argument?"

Had they argued? Not really. More like he'd told her he was moving and she'd verbalized that they were through.

"I heard he turned his notice in yesterday. I wasn't going to say anything until you did, but you've looked so miserable today that I couldn't hold it in any longer."

There it was. Confirmation that he was leaving. Everyone knew. Charlie was leaving her.

"I'm not sure what to say. My boyfriend—former boyfriend," she corrected, "is moving out of town. I was shocked by the news and haven't quite recovered."

Chrissie's expression pinched. "You didn't know?"

"You probably knew before I did."

Her friend's eyes widened. "He hadn't mentioned he was considering a move to Nashville?"

Savannah shook her head. "Not even a peep."

Chrissie looked blown away. "What was he thinking? He should have talked such a big decision over with you."

Maybe her expectations hadn't been unfounded if Chrissie thought the same thing as she had. What was she thinking? Of course he should have mentioned the possibility of a move. They'd been inseparable for months. Her anger was well founded.

"Apparently not."

"You said 'former boyfriend'," Chrissie pointed out. "You two are finished, then?"

Savannah had to fight to keep her hand from covering her lower abdomen. She and Charlie would never be finished. There would always be a tie that bound them.

A child that bound them.

Still, she didn't need him, would not allow herself to need him. Some fools never learned, but she wasn't going to fall into that category.

Toying with her stethoscope, she shrugged and told the truth. "Yeah, as a couple, we're finished."

Wincing, Charlie paused in the hallway. Neither woman had noticed him walking up behind them. Neither one knew he was overhearing their conversation.

Should he clear his throat or something?

He shouldn't feel guilty for eavesdropping. If they didn't want someone to overhear their conversation they shouldn't be having it in the middle of the CVICU hallway.

"I'm sorry to hear that," Chrissie told Savannah, giving her a quick hug. "I thought you two were perfect together."

Perfect together.

They had been perfect together, but wasn't that the way most relationships started? All happy faces and rainbows? It was what came along after the happy faces and rainbows faded that was the problem.

He was just leaving before the bright and shiny faded, before hell set in and people died.

Charlie absolutely was not going to be like his father.

If Rupert had been miserable at giving up his dream of a career in medicine, then he'd made Charlie's mother doubly so until her death in a car accident when Charlie had been fifteen. That had been after a particularly gruesome argument that Charlie had tried to stop. He'd never forgiven himself that he hadn't been able to protect her from his father. He'd tried, failed, and look what had happened, at what she'd done to escape his father—to escape him?

Guilt slammed him and he refused to let the memory take hold, instead focusing on events before that dreadful night. Why his parents had stayed together was beyond Charlie. They should have divorced.

They should never have married.

No doubt his mother would have been a hundred times better off if Rupert had walked away instead of marrying her and making her pay for her pregnancy every day for the rest of her life.

Regardless, Rupert had stayed with his wife and had instilled in Charlie the knowledge that giving up one's dreams for another person ultimately led to misery for all involved. His mother had seconded that motion, and when she'd died it had confirmed that her son was not worth living for. Charlie wasn't able to make another person happy, nor was he able to protect anyone from life's harsher realities. Those were lessons he'd learned well.

Thank goodness he was leaving before he'd sunk so far into his relationship with Savannah that he couldn't resurface.

That she couldn't resurface.

The next two months couldn't pass soon enough.

* * *

Savannah didn't have to turn to know that Charlie was behind her. Something inside always went a little haywire when he was near and, whatever that something was, it was sending out crazy signals.

"All good things must come to an end," she told her friend, not going into anything more specific, wishing she wasn't so aware of the man behind her.

With time, she wouldn't even remember who he was, she lied to herself, trying to balm the raw ache in her heart, trying to cling to her anger. Anger was easier than pain.

"You really aren't going to try to make a go of it long distance?"

She shook her head. "I don't do long distance relationships."

Perhaps, under the right circumstances, she would have, but nothing about what had happened with Charlie was right. He'd blindsided her and left her emotionally devastated.

Chrissie gave her a suspicious look. "You aren't going to leave Chattanooga on me, are you?"

She shook her head again. "Nope. Not that he offered to take me with him, but I'm not leaving Chattanooga to chase after a man or for any other reason. This is my home. If I'm not worth staying for, then good riddance."

She was pretty sure her words were aimed more at the man eavesdropping than at her friend. But what did it matter? Her words were true.

If only the truth didn't hurt so much. Didn't make her so angry. Not hurt. Angry.

"As your nurse supervisor, I'm glad to hear that. As your friend, I'm sad that you and Dr. Keele have split. You two seemed to have something very special and, quite frankly, I was more than a little envious."

Yeah, she'd thought so too.

"Appearances can be deceiving."

Very deceiving. She'd believed in him and his feelings for her. She'd been the one deceived and had no one to blame but her foolish, naïve self.

Only she blamed him, too.

Why had he acted so enamored if he wasn't? He'd treated her as if she was the candle that gave light to his world. They'd been together almost a year. A freaking year. A year of her life. A year of his life. Gone. Meaningless.

Only it wasn't.

Because there was a physical reminder of that year, of their relationship, growing inside her.

Darn him for taking the happiest day of her life and turning it into the worst.

She'd cried enough tears to sail a fleet upon, had to have used up all her tears, and yet, even now, she could spring a leak that would rival Old Faithful.

A man who would so easily walk away from her wasn't worth her heartache and tears.

"Speaking of the devil," she said, turning to let Charlie know she knew he was there. She wouldn't cry. Not in front of him. If she had her way, she'd never cry over him again. "Good afternoon, Dr. Keele."

He grimaced at her formal use of his name.

Good. He deserved a little grimacing after all she'd gone through the night before and every moment since. But, seriously, what had he expected? A smile and, *Glad to see you*?

"I imagine you're here to see Mr. Roberts. He's in Room 336 and, although he's still going in and out of atrial fibrillation, he's otherwise stable on the IV medication since his admission this morning."

All business. She could do it. She would do it.

No matter that he used to smile at her with his whole being and make her feel like the most precious person in the world.

No matter that two nights ago he'd kissed her all

over and done crazily amazing things to her body and held her tightly afterwards.

No matter that his baby was nestled deep inside her body.

No matter that he'd utterly ripped her heart to shreds the night before, forever destroying her faith in him. In them.

No matter that she might just hate him for what he'd done.

He was leaving.

They were no longer a couple.

She no longer looked at him with rose-colored glasses.

He was a doctor. She was a nurse. She could play that game and keep things professional for as long as she had to.

She could hold her emotions in, keep her expression detached. He didn't deserve to see her pain.

He'd be gone in two months and then letting him see her hurt would be the least of her worries.

This was how it had to be, Charlie reminded himself as he went to check on his patient.

But to look into the eyes of the woman he'd spent the past year of his life with and see nothing but cold disdain—that he hadn't been prepared for.

He should have been. He'd known they were going to end the moment he'd told her he was leaving. He'd expected her anger. Maybe her yelling and screaming at him would have been easier than the look of disdain. He'd lived with both, growing up. The yelling, the screaming at how worthless he was, the looks of hatred.

Yet seeing that look on Savannah's face gutted him.

He examined the unconscious man, checking the readouts on his telemetry, making note of adjustments he'd make to his care.

Hopefully, tomorrow they'd be able to decrease his sedation and start weaning him off his respiratory ventilator.

He heard someone enter the room behind him, but knew it wasn't Savannah. She gave off a vibe that caused his insides to hum when she was near and he wasn't humming. Not even the slightest little buzz.

"Do I need to reassign your patients?"

He turned to look at the nurse supervisor, then shook his head. "I'll be here for two months and plan to take care of my patients during that time."

She arched a brow at his obvious misunderstanding. "Savannah taking care of your patients won't be a problem?"

"Not for me." He put his stethoscope back in his scrub pocket, then got a squirt of antimicrobial solution. Almost methodically, he rubbed his hands until the wet solution dissipated. He tried to appear casual when he asked, "Did she ask to be reassigned?"

Chrissie shook her head. "She'd never do that. She's way too professional, no matter what her personal feelings are."

He met the woman's gaze. "Then we shouldn't be having this conversation."

Chrissie didn't back down. If anything, his stern look had her hiking up her chin to take advantage of every bit of her still short stature. "That's probably true, but it's my job to make sure everything goes smoothly on this unit. I don't want any unforeseen problems cropping up and I'm taking a proactive approach to this potential situation."

"As far as I'm concerned, there is no potential situation. I'll be gone in two months."

Her dark eyes narrowed but, rather than say anything negative, she surprised him by saying, "Congratulations on your new job. I hear it was a nice promotion."

"Thank you. It was."

She hesitated a moment, then looked him square in the eyes. "You're sure that's really what you want, though?"

He frowned. "Of course it is. It's a very prestigious position."

"Hard to have a conversation with a prestigious position over the dinner table."

She thought he was a fool for accepting the greatest career opportunity he'd been presented with because of Savannah. Let her think that. He didn't care what she thought—what anyone thought. He knew he'd made the right decision. That he was doing what was best for Savannah by destroying her feelings for him.

Feigning that her look of pity didn't faze him, he shrugged. "I won't be lonely."

She gave him a disappointed look. "No, I don't imagine you will. Congrats again, Dr. Keele. I hope you find whatever it is you're looking for in Nashville."

"I'm not looking for anything in Nashville," he told her retreating back. He wasn't looking for anything anywhere.

Charlie grabbed hold of the bed rail and stared down at his unconscious patient for long moments.

Taking the Nashville job had been the right thing for all involved.

What hadn't been the right thing had been getting so involved with someone. He wouldn't make that mistake again.

That might not be a problem anytime in the near future anyway. The thought of anyone other than Savannah just didn't appeal.

How was any other woman supposed to compare to the way she lit up a room just by walking into it? To the way her smile reached her eyes and he knew what she was thinking without her saying a word? How she enjoyed the same things he did, shared his love of Civil War history and taking long hikes up on Lookout Mountain on the battlefield? To running with him at dawn along the Tennessee River near her apartment?

The reality was no woman ever had measured up to Savannah and he suspected they never would. The thought of sharing his days, his nights, with anyone other than her left him cold.

She was perfect and he wanted her to stay that way.

Leaving was the best thing he could do for all involved.

CHAPTER THREE

"CODE BLUE. CODE BLUE."

Savannah rushed to the patient's room. Her patient had just flatlined.

She'd been in the bathroom when the call came over the intercom.

She hated that, but her bladder didn't hold out the way it used to. A symptom of her pregnancy, she supposed.

Chrissie was in the room performing CPR when Savannah got there with the crash cart. The man was on a ventilator so she was only performing chest compressions and the machine breathed for him, giving him oxygen.

Charlie rushed in right behind Savannah. A unit secretary was there acting as a recorder of all the events of the code.

"Give him some epi," Charlie ordered, taking charge of the code, as was his position.

Savannah did so, then prepared the defibrillator machine, attached the leads to the man's chest.

"All clear," Charlie ordered and everyone stepped away from the man.

Savannah pushed the button to activate the defibrillator.

The man's body gave a jerk and his heart did a few abnormal beats.

"Let me know the second it's recharged," Charlie ordered, having taken over the chest compressions for Chrissie.

"Now," Savannah told him.

"All clear," he warned.

As soon as everyone had stepped back, Savannah hit the button, sending another electrical shock through the man's body.

His heart did a wild beat then jumped back into a beating rhythm. Not a normal one, but one that would sustain life for the moment.

"I'm going to take him into the cardiac lab. He needs an ablation of the abnormal AV node, a pacemaker, and a permanent defibrillator put in STAT."

"Yes, sir."

By this time, other staff had entered the room and a transport guy and Savannah wheeled the patient toward the cardiac lab, Charlie beside them.

Chrissie called the lab, told them of the emergency situation and that Dr. Keele was on his way with his patient.

Savannah helped to get the patient settled in the surgical lab, then turned to go.

"Savannah?"

Slowly, she turned toward Charlie, met eyes she'd once loved looking into. Now, she just wanted him to hurry up and leave.

He searched her face for something, but she couldn't be sure what, just that his expression looked filled with regret. That she understood. She had regrets. Dozens of them. Hundreds. All centering around him.

She'd been so stupid.

"You did a great job back there," he finally said, although his words fell flat.

She swallowed back the nausea rising in her throat and wanted to scream. They were broken up. He shouldn't be being nice. And if he said, *Let's just be friends*, it might be him needing resuscitation because she might just choke him out.

Rather than answer, she gave him a squint-eyed glare, then turned to go.

When she got outside the lab, she leaned against the cold concrete wall and fought crumbling.

Fought throwing up. Fought curling into a fetal position and letting loose the pain inside her.

Two months.

She could do anything for two months.

Only, really, wasn't she just fooling herself every time she thought *two months*?

Wasn't she really looking at the rest of her life because, with the baby growing inside her, she'd have a permanent connection to Charlie?

A permanent connection she'd been so happy about, but now—now she wasn't sure. How could she be happy about a baby when the father didn't want her?

Would he want their child?

When was she supposed to tell him? Before he left? After he left? Before the baby got here? After the baby got here?

Never?

He'd find out. They shared too many friends. Nashville wasn't that far away. Not telling him wasn't an option, even if she could keep the news from him. She couldn't live with that secret. On the off chance that he would want a relationship with their child, she had to tell him.

Would he think she'd purposely tried to trap him into staying? See her news as her trying to manipulate him? Would he understand that she didn't want him to stay because she was pregnant when he hadn't been willing to stay for her? That he'd destroyed the magic that had been between them forever?

She lightly banged her head against the concrete wall.

What was she going to do?

A month later, Charlie shifted the box of Savannah's belongings to where he could free up a hand to knock on her apartment door.

And stood there, frozen.

Why wasn't he knocking?

Why was he just standing outside her apartment like some kind of crazy man?

He was crazy.

She'd texted him earlier that day and asked what he wanted her to do with his things. He couldn't really recall what he had at her place, other than his running gear and ear buds and maybe a few odds and ends, some clothes. Maybe, instead of saying he'd stop by and pick up his things, he should have told her to just keep it all.

But that still left him with having to deal with her belongings. She'd had some toiletries in his bathroom and some clothes that he'd boxed up. So, tonight, he'd kill two birds with one stone. Or something like that. Because he'd stripped his place of all physical reminders of Savannah and taped them inside the box. Out of sight, out of mind.

Not really—forgetting Savannah would come with time.

As he'd been driving to her place, the night he'd told Savannah about his new job kept replaying through his mind. Over and over.

She'd been so happy when she'd met him at the door, had told him she had good news. Good news she'd never gotten to share because he'd told his news first and all hell had broken loose.

She hated him. He saw it in her eyes on the rare occasion when their eyes met at the hospital. She no longer wanted anything to do with him.

Mission accomplished.

Earlier that day he'd run into her and gotten a good look. She'd been abrupt, to the point, immediately launching into a report about one of his patients. Darkness had shadowed her eyes. Her face had been devoid of the happy sparkle that had always shone so brightly. She'd looked so completely opposite to how she'd been a month ago that her greeting him at the door, her smile, her giddiness,

the warmth of her kiss and hug, had played on repeat in his head.

What had caused her such joy a month ago?

Him? Yes, they had had a good relationship, but
only because he'd never had any expectations of
her, had never made any promises that he'd live to
break.

Hand poised at the door, he closed his eyes.

He couldn't do this. He didn't feel up to being
the jerk he needed to be. He needed her to keep
hating him, to move on. Instead, he just wanted to
ask her what her good news had been, to see joy
in her eyes.

He could never do either. He came with too much
baggage, too much risk.

What if he pushed Savannah as far as he'd pushed
his mother? What if the same type of thing happened?

He turned to go.

Fighting the urge to slam the apartment door she'd
just opened back shut, Savannah stared at the man
in the hallway with his back to her. At the sound
of the door opening, he turned toward her. His
eyes were full of raw emotion and she thought she
should definitely slam the door and bolt it closed.

"My neighbor called and told me you were loitering in the hallway," she said as explanation for why she'd opened the door since he hadn't knocked. "She wanted to know if she should call the police."

"What did you tell her?"

"To call them," she said, even though they both knew it wasn't true. "That I hoped they'd lock you up and throw away the key."

"I thought that might have been your answer."

She raised an eyebrow and waited. Just as he could wait if he thought she was going to invite him into her apartment. She wasn't.

She'd been nauseated most of the day, but had made the mistake of eating dinner anyway because she knew she needed to eat to keep the baby healthy. Her grilled cheese wasn't sitting well in her stomach. Charlie showing up at her apartment wasn't helping.

"You looked as if you weren't feeling well when I was at the hospital earlier," he pointed out as if this was breaking news.

"It's been a long month," she said, a mixture of adrenaline and exhaustion tugging at her body.

She was showing the patience of a saint by not screaming and yelling. She'd like to scream and yell. But, really, what good would that do? He was leaving. But, way beyond that, he'd pretty much put her in her place when she'd said he should have discussed such a big decision with her. That place hadn't been beside him or as someone who had any importance in his life.

That knowledge kept her in the middle of her doorway, staring at a man she'd once thought she'd spend her life growing old with.

"Are you just going to stand there not saying anything?" she asked, injecting as much annoyance as she could muster into her voice.

Glancing down the hallway as if he half expected the police to really show up, he shifted the box he held and raked his fingers through his dark hair. "I brought your stuff."

Her fingers itched to smooth out the ruffled tufts of thick hair left in the wake of his frustration, but she stayed them by tucking her hands into the pockets of her nursing scrubs.

"Fine," she huffed, not moving out of the doorway, almost afraid to move for fear of jostling where her dinner precariously sat in her belly. "Set it down there and I'll get your stuff so you can leave."

"I was leaving. You opened the door."

His frustration was palpable and had her shaking her head.

"You'd been in my hallway long enough that Mrs. Henry was having a conniption."

"She always was nosy."

"I thought you liked her."

"I did." He raked his fingers through his hair again. "I do."

Savannah winced. Two little words she'd once thought she'd hear him say, but under very different circumstances.

Unable to bear looking at him a moment longer, she turned away, put her hand to her lips to stay anything that might be going to come out.

"Are you okay?" he asked from behind her.

She gritted her teeth to keep from verbally attacking him. No need to have Mrs. Henry calling the police for real.

"I'm fabulous," she lied.

You could mend a broken heart back together, but it was never the same. She'd never be the same or look at Charlie the same.

That magic giddy bubble was popped forever.

She'd trusted in his feelings implicitly and he'd shattered that trust. He'd unilaterally made a decision that had torn apart what she'd thought had been a permanent relationship and he'd not had remorse or guilt or a sense that he should have talked with her first. Her complete misjudgment of that meant she would never allow herself to trust in her own feelings again. Not with Charlie or any other man. How could she when she'd been so completely wrong about Charlie?

Exhaustion gripped her body, making standing a challenge and all she could do. "Are you gone yet? Your stuff is by the door. Grab it and go."

She just wanted him to leave. But instead he stepped into her apartment. Maybe he'd get his stuff, then go.

"Tell me whatever your good news was."

Spinning to stare at him in disbelief, Savannah's stomach dropped. Her jaw did, too.

"Tell me whatever it was you wanted to tell me a month ago, Savannah."

For a brief moment she considered telling him. Right or wrong, she wasn't ready to share her news with him. She just didn't feel strong enough tonight to face whatever reaction he might have. Not tonight.

She squared her shoulders, lifted her chin, and tried to look as if she could successfully take on the world.

Normally, she could.

"Maybe you should have thought of that before you took a job two hours away," she tossed out.

"My taking a job two hours away has nothing to do with you," he insisted with more than a hint of annoyance.

Good. His words annoyed her, too.

And hurt. His words hurt. Deep and to the core.

"It should have," she said so softly she wasn't even sure he'd hear her.

"Says who?"

"Says me." She lifted her gaze to his and dared him to say otherwise.

His jaw worked back and forth and a visible struggle played on his face. "Why do you get to decide that it should have?"

"For the same reasons you got to decide that it didn't."

He let out a low breath. He stepped closer, stared down directly into her eyes. His gaze narrowed. "You think I should have said no to the position?"

Her stomach rumbled and she clenched the tips of her fingers into her palms. "That's not what I'm saying."

"Then what are you saying?"

"That I should have mattered enough for my opinion to have counted. I didn't."

He studied her for a few long seconds. "My career means everything to me." His tone was flat, almost cold. "I won't let anyone or anything stand in the way."

Ouch. There it was. The truth.

A truth she'd not understood because for the past year they'd obviously been on the same page. Sure, he worked hard and long hours, but so did she. Their jobs hadn't been an issue. Finding time to spend together hadn't been an issue.

She'd thought they'd been each other's priority. Obviously, in Charlie's case it was more a case of convenience than priority.

She'd been easy.

No, she hadn't. She'd not immediately fallen into bed with him. Not immediately. But too quickly. The attraction had been so strong. The sexual chemistry so magnetic.

Even now, with everything that had happened, with her body threatening to reject her evening meal, his nearness made her heart race, her breath quicken, her nipples tighten, her thighs clench. He made every sense come alive, made every nerve ending aware.

She hated it. Hated that even knowing she didn't mean what she'd thought she'd meant he had such power over her body.

He wasn't the man she'd thought he was—wasn't the man she'd fallen so hard for. That man had been an illusion. She'd fantasized and projected upon him. Maybe because of their strong sexual chemistry and her desire to believe the intensity of their lovemaking was due to something more than just physical attraction. Outdated of her, no doubt, but that had to be it.

She didn't know how she was going to handle her future, her baby's future, but at the moment one thing was very, very clear to her.

She looked Charlie straight in the eyes and felt an inner strength that surprised her. Sure, he'd probably always affect her physically. He was a good-looking, virile man who gave off an over-abundance of pheromones and her body remembered all too well the magic he wielded. But he'd destroyed the rose-colored glasses that she'd adoringly looked at him through. What she now saw wasn't worthy of what she'd been willing to give him.

"You don't belong here," she told him. "Not in my apartment. Not in my life."

Not ever again.

* * *

Savannah's words stung Charlie in places deep within his chest. Places that weren't supposed to be accessible to anyone, much less vulnerable to words that were all too reminiscent of those flung at him in the past.

He took a step back.

He wavered between wanting to beg her to forgive him and telling himself to walk away and forget her. She was right. He didn't belong. He'd never belonged. Never would.

He'd always known that. Had never been able to forget that until Savannah. Look at what that memory lapse had caused.

Looking exhausted, Savannah closed her eyes then turned her back to him and walked over to her sofa, where she sat down. "I don't feel up to doing this again, Charlie. I'm sorry, but I just don't."

Her skin had lost its color and she had crossed her arms over her belly.

"You look pale."

She didn't comment, just proceeded to turn a few more shades toward ghastly gray. Hands over her stomach, she leaned forward and made a noise that might have been a moan, but might have been a dry heave.

Despite not being invited in, he stepped further into her living room and toward the sofa. "Are you okay?"

Without looking up, she shook her head. "No, I am not okay. Get your stuff and leave."

He was torn. She wanted him to go. She really did. He could hear it in her voice. But how did he just walk out when she looked as if she was majorly ill?

Then she was.

With a panicked glance at him, she bolted off the sofa and toward the half bath just off the living room.

Worried, Charlie followed her to the small half bath, grabbed a rolled up washcloth from the basket that sat on the vanity, and ran cold water over it, all the while keeping his eyes trained on Savannah. She knelt over the toilet, gripping the sides and heaving out the contents of her stomach.

When he'd squeezed out the excess water, he folded the washcloth. He pulled her hair back away from her face, put the washcloth across her forehead, and helped support her while she leaned over the toilet.

He didn't say a word, just held the washcloth to her forehead, kept her hair back from her face, and felt torn into a million directions as to what he should do.

He couldn't leave her like this even if he wanted to.

He couldn't.

He didn't have it in him to walk away with her ill.

When her heaving seemed to have subsided, she glanced up at him with a tear-streaked face and he felt something in his chest squeeze painfully tight.

"I hate that you saw me like this."

Kneeling, he took the washcloth and gently wiped her mouth. "I'm a doctor, Savannah. I've seen worse."

A long sigh escaped her lips. "Not from me."

She looked lost, like a child, and more than anything he wanted to ease her distress and take care of her.

"I'm going to carry you to your room, help you change out of your scrubs, wash your face and brush your teeth, then put you to bed."

She closed her eyes for a moment then shook her head. "I don't need you. I can take care of myself."

"You're sick. Let me help you."

Her expression pinched, and he expected her to argue, but instead, her skin going gray again, she lowered her gaze. "No carrying. Just…just help me get to my room."

Charlie steadied her as she stood, wrapped his arms around her waist, and walked with her to her room. He stayed close until she seemed steady on her feet in front of her en suite sink, where she washed her face, then brushed her teeth. He went to her bedroom, opened a drawer and pulled out an oversized T-shirt.

His T-shirt.

How many nights had he watched her pull on this shirt after they'd made love? Sleepily, she'd smile at him, then curl back up in bed. He'd tuck her in with a kiss, and then head to his place feeling like a million bucks. He'd never see that love-laden smile again. Never be the one to kiss her goodnight. He squeezed the worn cotton material between his fingers, then shook off the moment of nostalgia.

She was better off without him. Just look at what had happened to his mother. He had his career. His career was what was important.

"Here." He held out the shirt through the bathroom door. "Put this on."

She glanced at his offering, then bit into her lower lip.

"I'll wait here while you change. If you feel sick again or need my help, call out. I'll be right there."

Taking the shirt, she nodded and shut the bathroom door.

The lock clicked and it echoed through his head that Savannah had forever closed off a part of herself to him.

As much as he tried to tell himself that was okay, as he sank onto the foot of her bed he wondered at his great sense of loss when going to Nashville was definitely for the best.

CHAPTER FOUR

FEELING PHYSICALLY BETTER after emptying her stomach but mortified, Savannah splashed cold water over her face.

She'd just thrown up in her bathroom with Charlie right there.

To give him credit, he'd been a champ, keeping her hair back and putting the cold cloth against her forehead. But she wasn't giving him credit. No way.

Wiping her hands on a towel, drying them, she then placed her palms over her lower abdomen.

Oh, God. What was she going to do?

How was she going to explain vomiting?

She'd known for a month now and hadn't told him.

She studied her reflection—the pale skin, the tired eyes, the tension tugging at her features.

Why hadn't she told him?

Because he didn't deserve to know?

Maybe telling him would be punishment because he didn't want children, didn't want any ties to her.

Was it fear that really held her back?

The fear that, although she loved this baby no matter what, she might be on her own raising their child? She'd be fine. Just look at what a great job Chrissie was doing with Joss. Savannah could rock the single mom thing, too.

"You okay in there?"

She closed her eyes, unable to stand the reflection staring back at her a moment longer.

"Savannah?"

"I'm fine."

That wasn't true. Not really. And they both knew it, although he had no clue as to the real reason.

Charlie moved toward the bathroom door the moment it opened, staying close to Savannah's side as she came out of the bathroom.

"Let me help you into bed."

"I don't want to go to bed," she protested.

"You look awful. You need to be in bed."

She glared at him. "Good to know. Thanks."

"You know what I mean." He fought the urge to roll his eyes.

"Fine, then—I don't want to go to bed," she reiterated, shaking off his hand as he reached for her arm.

"Do you have to argue with everything I say these days?"

"No, but there's no reason for me to go to bed."

"Other than the fact you worked a twelve-hour shift, look dead on your feet, and you just threw up?"

"Yeah, other than that." She looked ready to drop. Possibly her illness was related to exhaustion, but it was just as possible his presence had led to her sickness.

"You make me sick."

He winced at the words from his past, shook them off, and focused on the fragile-looking woman in front of him.

He let out an exasperated sigh. "At least lie down and rest a few minutes while I clean your bathroom."

"Go home. It's not going to hurt if a used washcloth sits on the countertop overnight."

"I want to help you, Savannah. Let me." He did want to help. He wanted her smiling and happy, not miserable and sick.

Maybe he was destined to have a negative impact on anyone close to him. To make anyone unfortunate enough to get close to him miserable.

She glanced toward the doorway leading out into

the hallway, then sighed. Her remaining energy hissed out like a deflating balloon and she sat down on the edge of the bed. "I feel guilty letting you clean when I'm perfectly capable."

He'd really like to hold her, to stroke her hair, whisper words of comfort and stay with her until she felt better. It wasn't his place to do any of those things. Not anymore.

"If you looked perfectly capable I wouldn't have offered. You don't, so go to bed."

Surprisingly, she nodded and laid down on top of the comforter.

"I'll straighten your guest bathroom then be back to check on you."

Asking her to get into her bed struck him as odd. How many times had he gotten into that bed with her?

Odd to think he never would again.

That he'd lost that right.

That privilege.

Once he was in Nashville, had started his new job, made new friends, his having made the right decision would be reinforced. It was only because he was still here, still confronted every day with the life he'd become used to sharing with Savannah, that he was struggling.

Savannah would be much better off once he was gone and she could move on with her life. He blamed himself for allowing their relationship to go on for so long. He should have stepped away long ago, for Savannah's sake if not his own.

Then again, that was part of the problem, wasn't it? He should have protected her from ever getting close enough to him to feel broken-hearted.

Not that his track record for protecting those close to him was anything to brag about. Quite the opposite.

Once he'd straightened her bathroom, he went back to her bedroom and wasn't surprised to find her asleep.

She hadn't planned on going to sleep as she was still lying on top of the comforter rather than beneath it. Savannah was one of those that even if it were a hundred degrees outside she had to at least have a sheet over her. The fact she had dozed off spoke volumes as to how ill she was.

He should have asked if she needed anything.

He should have checked her temperature or something.

He was a cardiologist, not an infectious disease guy, but she probably had a stomach virus. Hopefully, it would run its course within twenty-four hours and she'd feel better soon.

He went back into the living room, grabbed a throw blanket off the sofa, and put it over her. She snuggled into the comfort of the blanket, but her breathing pattern didn't change to indicate that she'd awakened.

Charlie stood over the bed watching her for a few minutes. He'd told her she looked awful, but the truth was she was the most beautiful woman he'd ever known.

Fearing he might wake her but unable to resist, he ran his fingers over her forehead, brushing back a stray strand of long red hair and gauging her temperature at the same time. That was why he was touching her. To check her temperature. To see if she were physically ill. Not because he'd longed to touch the creamy perfection of her skin, to trace over the faint laugh lines at the corners of her eyes, the high angle of her cheekbones, the pert lines of her jaw.

To check her temperature.

No fever. That was good.

But she hadn't thrown up because she felt great. Something was definitely wrong.

Which left him in a quandary. Did he go or did he stay?

Tomorrow was Saturday and he wasn't on call this weekend. He'd planned to drive to Nashville in the morning to make a decision on living arrangements. Savannah wasn't on duty either, as he'd checked her schedule earlier that day.

No, he hadn't checked her schedule.

He'd just happened to glance at the nursing schedule and he'd just happened to note that she wasn't working that weekend.

What he wanted was to crawl up into the bed beside her, to hold her close and be there in case she needed him.

But he wouldn't. He couldn't be soft where she was concerned. Not even if she was sick.

But he wasn't leaving. That much he knew.

He eyed the empty side of the bed where he'd laid dozens of times. He had no rights where Savannah was concerned.

Which was something he suspected would haunt him a lot longer than he cared to admit.

He'd stay the night and be there if Savannah got sick again, would be there if she needed anything. Then he'd go back to being the world's biggest jerk.

* * *

Savannah woke with a start, stretched her arms above her head, then realized her living room throw was tucked around her.

Everything from the night before came rushing back. Charlie. Getting sick. His putting her to bed.

She glanced at her alarm clock. It was early. Much earlier than she'd like to be awake on a Saturday. But at least her stomach wasn't churning as it had been the night before.

At least, not yet.

So far, every day this week, she'd had mild nausea in the mornings that had escalated throughout the day and peaked in the evenings. Leave it to her to have such oddly timed "morning" sickness.

But other than the woes of her breakup with Charlie, her nausea, and some fatigue, she felt good. She had a doctor's appointment in two weeks and supposed she'd find out then how she was really doing. Until then, she'd take her prenatal vitamins and just take each day as it came.

She got out of bed, went to the bathroom, brushed her teeth, then left her room to go to the kitchen to get a glass of water and a couple of crackers in hopes of warding off nausea later in the day.

The moment she stepped into the open floor plan

of her living room/dining room/kitchen, her gaze landed on the man draped across her sofa. He was too long for it and looked horribly uncomfortable.

But there was also a peace on his face as he slept.

A peace she hadn't seen over the past few weeks.

Because, despite how much he'd devastated her with his decision, Charlie wasn't walking around ecstatic either. Actually, every time she'd seen him he looked stressed, tense.

She stared at him way longer than she should have, studying his features, yet again wondering if their child would look like him.

Lord, she hoped so.

Yet did she really want a constant reminder of the man who'd broken her heart?

Their child would be a constant reminder regardless of who he or she looked like.

She'd been right about one thing. The rest of her life was going to be entangled with Charlie's. Not in the way she'd dreamed, but they would share a bond.

Because of that bond, she'd eventually have to make peace with him, would have to figure out how to just be his friend or his acquaintance or whatever it was they were destined to be.

They were going to be parents together.

Savannah got her water, went back to her room, and crawled beneath the comforter, all too aware that a month ago Charlie would have been in bed beside her and she'd have snuggled up against him. Now, she had no right to touch him, no right to snuggle next to him.

Not that she wanted him in her bed. She didn't. She was just fine by herself. Better than fine.

She didn't need him. Only…

Tears came quicker than they should have, but eventually she dozed back into sleep.

"I wasn't sure what you'd feel like eating this morning, if anything, so I made you a few choices."

Stretching in her bed, Savannah blinked at the man carrying in a tray of food. "You cooked for me?"

Not meeting her eyes, he nodded. "It's not much, but I went with what I could find."

Which was pretty limited. Eating had been a chore the past week and she'd not bothered going to the grocery store. She'd made sure to eat a small healthy meal each evening, but otherwise she'd been grabbing food from work.

"I'm surprised you found anything at all."

She eyed the scrambled eggs, toast, oatmeal that

had to be made from an instant package, small glass of juice, and another that had water. "Looks good, but you shouldn't have."

Really, he shouldn't have. She needed to stay angry with him. Anger was so much better than the alternative emotions running rampant through her.

Setting the tray on the bed, he studied her. "You look better this morning. You got really pale last night. Virus?"

Now was the time to tell him the truth. He'd given her the perfect opening to tell him about their baby. Only she couldn't find the words that early in the morning to tell him. She tried. She opened her mouth but the words didn't come out, no matter how hard she tried to force them out.

"I'm not sure if anything's been going around the hospital or not," he continued, studying her as if he were gauging how she was going to react to him this morning. "Nothing on the cardiac unit, at any rate."

"Hopefully it will stay that way." Those words had come out just fine. Why hadn't the others? One simple two-word sentence was all she needed. *I'm pregnant.* She eyed the food and her stomach growled. She picked up a piece of toast, took a bite, and was grateful it settled happily into her stomach. She ate slowly, but felt better than she had all week. Hopefully that was a good sign that she wasn't going to be as nauseated.

"What are your plans for the day?"

She shrugged. "I'm not sure."

"I'm headed to Nashville to look at a couple of apartment complexes. I'm pretty sure I'm going to lease one of them, based on online reviews and a virtual tour, but wanted to take a look at a few others before committing."

Yeah, he wasn't so good at committing.

Which probably wasn't fair since he'd never given her any reason to think he would commit, other than just be in a relationship with her for a year and treat her as if she was his every desire. Which was good enough reason, right?

"Do you want to go with me?"

Her head shot up. He looked as surprised as she felt, then his face took on a remorseful appearance.

"You threw up last night and here I am trying to put you in a car for four plus hours today. I wasn't thinking."

No, he hadn't because he obviously regretted the invitation.

"I am feeling better this morning. I'm not nauseated." Not that the idea of four hours in a car appealed to her, but she did have news she needed to tell him. Maybe being trapped in a car with him would help her find the right words to tell him that she was having his baby.

Although she probably shouldn't be bragging too much about not being nauseated because this was the first morning in over a week that she'd not felt at least a little ill.

"I don't have other plans so I guess I could go with you."

He looked torn at her answer and for a moment she thought he was going to take back the invitation.

No worries, Charlie, she silently assured him. *I'm not going to beg you to change your mind about us. We are through.*

But on the way home from Nashville would be the perfect opportunity to tell him the truth. Not with the fun little baby items she'd bought the day she'd done the pregnancy test. Not with any cute little reveal ideas she'd looked at online. Just the blunt facts while he was trapped in a car with her so they could discuss the ramifications of the fact they were going to be parents.

"What do you think?" Charlie asked Savannah as she walked through the last apartment they were looking at. He couldn't believe she was there with him. The invitation had slipped out of his mouth and when she'd agreed he hadn't been able to bring himself to withdraw it.

"They're all nice." She sounded almost bored.

"But?"

"The first one we looked at seems the most practical. With being on Twenty-First Avenue, it's close to the hospital and I like its layout the best. It doesn't have much of a yard available, but you don't really need a yard. Centennial Park isn't that far if you felt the need for grass beneath your feet."

"That's the one I liked best, too." It was part of a small apartment complex that housed ten units. She was right that there wasn't much of a yard, but that wasn't a deal-breaker.

She averted her gaze, not wanting him to see whatever he'd see in her eyes. She supposed she would visit him there at some point. They'd be sharing custody of their baby.

Not that the baby would be able to be away from her for the first year, as she intended to breastfeed. But there would come a point in time where she'd be dropping her child off to Charlie for them to spend time together.

Sadness hit her. Just the thought of being away

from her child unnecessarily made her heart ache. Made her all the more angry at Charlie, at herself, that she'd put so much stock into their relationship.

"I'm going to go back there so I can sign the appropriate papers and get this checked off my to-do list."

"Is it a long list?"

"Long enough. Moving isn't easy. Haven't you ever moved, Savannah?" He sounded incredulous that she might not have.

"Sure, but only from home to college, then into my apartment after graduation."

"You always lived alone?"

"Nope. I had a roommate in the dorm and one when I first moved into the apartment. She got married and I just never replaced her." That had been right before Charlie had come into her life.

She sat in the car while he ran in to sign the forms at the apartment complex, then they grabbed a meal at a restaurant a friend had told him about. Amazingly, Savannah's stomach held out okay, but she ordered fairly bland just in case.

Their conversation ranged from awkward to relaxed when they'd forget their new status for a few minutes, then back to awkward when they remembered.

Savannah's heart ached and she had to remind herself of why she was there—not to make nice with Charlie, but so she could tell him about their baby on the drive home.

But by the time they got into the car, her head pounded and she closed her eyes. She couldn't tell him. Not like this. Not in a car, when things felt so wrong. Not until after her doctor's appointment and she knew more details.

Not until she could handle whatever reaction he might have.

"You'll understand if I don't invite you in," Savannah said, her fingers clutching the car door handle.

Charlie frowned. He hadn't planned on going in. Getting some space between him and Savannah was what he needed. Still, something in her tone irked him and he found himself saying, "You should invite me in. We could have a good last month together, Savannah."

She gave him a horrified look. "You mean sex?"

She made the word sound like it should have four letters and he pushed on. He needed to destroy whatever glimmers of feeling she still had for him.

"You can't deny it," he said with a tone so smooth

it almost disgusted him. He could only imagine how dirty it made Savannah feel.

"You were more to me than sex, Charlie."

Were. As in past tense. Which was how it needed to be. She needed to find someone who could protect her and give her a fairy tale. Too bad the thought of her with someone else made his blood boil.

"I could make you feel good." He raked his gaze over her. "That hasn't changed and we both know it."

"Everything's changed."

He wanted to argue that some things would never change, but then realized what he'd be admitting if he said that. Did he believe he was going to spend the rest of his life wanting this woman? Missing this woman?

To think that was foolishness. They'd both move on—her to someone who deserved her, him to his career. She deserved so much better.

He was to blame for her misery. No surprise there. He'd been making people miserable since before his birth. So much so his own mother had preferred death to him.

Savannah hesitated on opening the handle, looking indecisive, but, without another word, she opened the door and disappeared into her apartment complex, leaving him to wonder what she'd been considering saying.

"Goodbye, Savannah," he said to his empty car and drove away without a backward glance. She was right. Everything had changed.

CHAPTER FIVE

"HER ECHOCARDIOGRAM SHOWED an ejection fraction of fifteen percent, but apparently that is an old finding and related to a myocardial infarction she suffered three years ago. She's here because the defibrillator she had put in at that time keeps going off, causing her to lose consciousness."

Charlie studied Savannah as she kept her voice professional and monotone, just as she had at every other point their paths had crossed over the past two months.

"Defibrillator malfunction?" he asked.

"The ER doctor who admitted her didn't think so. She's been in and out of ventricular tachycardia since arriving. He started her on—" she named the medication "—which has stopped the defibrillator from firing, but her shortness of breath is worse."

"That's why you called me?"

Her lips pressed into a thin line, displaying her annoyance with his question.

"Her heart rate has stayed in the low sixties and

her blood pressure on the low side of normal, but when I assess her I know something is spiraling downhill."

He wasn't familiar with Iva Barton. He was taking the call for one of the other cardiologists, who'd squeezed in a vacation prior to Charlie's last day.

Which was quickly approaching.

Just one more day and he'd be in Nashville.

He and a couple of friends had moved his personal items last weekend. He was leaving most of his furniture to stage his house and had signed the real estate agreement just this week. Everything was happening fast.

Like the seconds ticking away with Savannah staring at him in question because he'd not commented on her assessment.

"I'll go check her."

"Thank you." Relief flickered across her face. Had she thought he wouldn't?

"Come with me?"

She looked hesitant, then shrugged. "Okay, Dr. Keele."

He could almost smile at the way she'd let him know she was only going with him because doing so was her duty. Fine, he was only asking in his professional capacity. He'd soon be gone. Asking her to come wasn't going to hurt a thing.

A pale woman in her early seventies lay in the hospital bed with multiple lines and telemetry wires attached to her frail body. Her gaze went to his the minute he entered the room, as if she wondered what poking and prodding he'd be doing.

"Hello, Mrs. Barton. You already know this, but Dr. Richards, your regular cardiologist, is out of town, so you're stuck with me. Your nurse has been filling me in. Sounds like you've had quite the day. How are you feeling?"

She grimaced. "Like I was kicked in the chest."

"When did that start?"

"When my defibrillator went off this morning." The white-haired woman clutched at her thin chest, rubbing across her sternum. "I haven't felt right since."

"Dr. Richards had scheduled her to see an electrophysiologist, thinking her defibrillator wasn't working correctly," a woman in her early thirties said from the chair next to the hospital bed. "Her appointment was actually scheduled for tomorrow, but then it went off this morning and she passed out. I called for an ambulance to come get her."

"You did the right thing," he assured the concerned woman, obviously the patient's daughter, then turned back to his patient. "Your heart is weak and your tests show that your defibrillator is going off because your heart keeps going out of rhythm. That's why you've been feeling funny."

"Why has my rhythm changed?"

"There are lots of things that can do it, but most likely it's due to the large chunk of damaged cardiac muscle from your heart attack a few years ago. Your body is working hard to try to compensate for that loss, but not doing so well. I've looked over what tests you've previously had at Chattanooga Memorial and the ones from the emergency room this morning. I'd like to schedule you for a viability test. I think a mechanical heart pump called a LVAD would be of benefit to ease the workload of your heart and increase your ejection fraction."

"Dr. Richards mentioned that to me at my last office visit, but said we needed to figure out this rhythm thing first." The woman glanced toward her daughter, then said, "I think my defibrillator is malfunctioning."

"From the way your rhythm looks, I'd say the defibrillator was doing exactly what it's supposed to and saving your life."

The young woman next to the bed stood, took her mother's hand. "What do we need to do?"

"We'll get the further testing done and go from there as to our next step."

When they stepped out of the ICU room, Savannah pinned him. "You think an LVAD is going to solve her problem?"

"Only one of them. I'd bet money she needs a ventricular ablation to correct that rhythm. The sooner the better."

"You want me to get the tests ordered?"

He nodded. "Once we get that and she's stable, we'll talk about transferring her to the heart failure team at Vanderbilt."

Savannah's face paled at the mention of where he would be transferring to himself. "Drumming up some business?"

"They are cutting edge when it comes to LVADs."

She didn't say anything.

"You should know that I do what's right for my patient. Always."

"Just not your girlfriend."

He frowned. She'd barely spoken to him since their Nashville trip, had gone out of her way to avoid him. The past month hadn't been easy, but he'd done it. Had even made a point to repeatedly go out with friends, knowing Savannah would catch wind of it and that it would fuel her dislike.

"Get the tests entered into Mrs. Barton's chart," he ordered as if he had no heart. "I'm going to make some calls to get everything started."

"Yes, sir." She said it so formally he had to look to make sure she hadn't saluted him. He wasn't so sure she hadn't.

What was he doing standing outside Savannah's apartment door again? Charlie wondered later that night.

Hadn't they said everything that needed to be said?

Apparently not or he wouldn't be here. With gifts.

Which seemed rather ridiculous, considering, but she'd always admired the vase. An interior decorator had chosen it, but Savannah had always been drawn to the intricate cut glass. The tickets, well, it wasn't as if he needed tickets to an upcoming Chattanooga concert. He'd bought them because she liked the band. It only seemed fitting he give them to her.

He heard her pause on the other side of the door, no doubt to glance through the peephole.

"No one's home," she called through the door.

"I have something for you."

"A going away present?" Sarcasm dripped from each word. "Isn't that supposed to be the other way around?"

"I have everything I need." He hoped his words rang with truth. He wasn't really sure, but he did know what Savannah needed. More importantly, what she didn't need. "Tomorrow's my last day at the hospital. What I have to say won't take a minute. Hurry up before Mrs. Henry calls the law."

He heard a thud. If he had to guess what had made it, he'd say she'd lightly banged her head against the door. After a few seconds, he heard the chain jingle and saw the door open.

Savannah stood there in yoga pants, an oversized T-shirt that hung from her body, and her hair pulled up in a ponytail. She didn't have a speck of make-up on, nor did she need it.

Or maybe she did because when he looked closer he noticed dark circles beneath her eyes that used to not be there.

"You look tired. If I did this to you, I'm sorry." More so than he'd ever be able to convey. The last thing he'd ever want was to hurt Savannah, but wasn't that part of the problem? He always hurt those he got close to.

"You didn't. I did it to myself."

He wasn't sure he understood what she meant, but she stepped aside to let him enter the apartment. He didn't hesitate to enter, for fear she might change her mind.

She shut the door, but made no move to go further into the apartment, just stood near the door as if she might fling it open and tell him to leave at any moment.

"I'm leaving for Nashville tomorrow after work. I felt I should come by before I left."

"You owe me nothing." Something on her face said she didn't believe that.

Maybe he didn't either and that was why he was there.

"You and I had a good time together. I'm sorry we ended under less than ideal circumstances."

Her lower lip disappeared between her teeth.

"I brought you this." He held out the vase. "You always admired it."

"You'll understand if I refuse."

Yeah, maybe he did understand. Still, he wanted her to have it. What she did with it after he was gone was up to her, even if it was to smash it into a thousand pieces.

"Then I guess you can toss it after I leave. There

are two tickets to go see that band you like stuck inside. Maybe you can take Chrissie or whomever you replace me with." He moved over to a shelf and set it down in an open spot, started to turn back toward her, then realized why the spot was open.

Because the photo of them at Lookout Mountain was gone.

He must have lingered long enough that she realized what he was staring at, because she moved from the door and came to stand next to him.

"I don't want the tickets any more than I want the vase."

"I've no use for them, Savannah." He turned to face her, was struck again by how fragile she appeared. Unable to resist, he brushed his fingers over her face, smoothing back a few stray hairs. The feel of her skin beneath his fingertips branded him with a thousand memories of touching her face, of touching her body, of holding her tight while the world ceased around them.

"I want you to have the tickets. I bought them for you."

Not meeting his eyes, she trembled beneath his fingers.

He needed to leave. He'd done what he came to do.

"I miss you, Savannah." God, he hated making

that admission, sure he hadn't meant to. The words had jumped from him, unbidden but true.

Her gaze lifted to his and she put her hand over his. Warmth at her touch burned through him.

His heart squeezed in his chest so tightly he thought it might pop. Part of him longed to take her into his arms and promise her anything she wanted just so long as she'd keep touching him. There were too many reasons for him to go for him to do that.

Her eyes locked with his, she moved closer.

He swallowed. Hard. She was so close he could feel her body heat, could feel his already pitiful defenses melting away.

Her gaze darted to the movement at his throat, then her lips grazed his neck.

Groaning, he closed his eyes, knowing he was about to give in to the very real need within him. His lips covered hers and his body sighed with re-lief, with recognition of the woman kissing him. He had missed her. So very much.

Her taste. Her smell. The feel of her. Everything.

Over and over, long lingering kisses full of des-peration.

"I want you so much, Savannah."

One last time he wanted to know what it felt to

be loved by her. Selfish, but he wasn't capable of stopping of his own free will. She should stop him, should push him away, for her own sake. But she didn't say anything, just ran her palms over his shoulders and pulled his shirt free of his pants, perhaps wanting one more time herself. She slid her fingers beneath the material. His muscles contracted.

No one had ever made his body react the way Savannah had. It was as if she had his nerve endings on a puppet string and could make them dance and sing any way she pleased.

Oh, how she pleased.

Her hands, her mouth, her body. He was a goner.

Maybe he'd been a goner from the beginning.

Whatever she wanted was hers. Fortunately, she didn't ask him to make promises. She didn't say anything at all, just stripped off his shirt in a few quick moves.

Her eyes ate him up, devouring what she'd uncovered and making him hard in the process. She wanted him. It was a heady sensation to look into her eyes and see that desire burn.

Why she was touching him, kissing him, now, he wasn't going to question; he would just count his lucky stars, knowing it was probably something similar to his own reasons.

He'd needed one last time.

Savannah knew she was crazy. Certifiable.

But it didn't matter.

Nothing mattered except this moment. In this moment she was going to take what she wanted. Charlie.

She shouldn't. She knew that. But, really, what did it matter? Tomorrow night he'd be gone and she'd be alone.

Until she told him the truth.

That thought gave her a moment's pause, but he scooped her into his arms and carried her to her bedroom, all the while kissing her mouth as if he couldn't bear not to and she pushed aside her flash of hesitation.

For now she could pretend it was real, that when morning came reality wouldn't set in. It would. She acknowledged that. But, for the moment, she was going to exist in that make-believe world because in the real world, even if he said all the right things, he couldn't undo the damage from the past two months and she wanted this one last time.

* * *

Hot, covered in sweat, heart pounding, body satiated, Charlie collapsed on top of Savannah.

His weight must have been too much for her because she wiggled and pushed at him.

"Sorry," he said, rolling over onto his side.

"For?"

"Squashing you."

"Oh, that." She waved off his concern and the hand he went to hold her with. She glanced around at the tangled bed sheets. "We shouldn't have done this."

"You wanted me as much as I wanted you," he reminded her.

"I'm not denying it. You know how to make my body do miraculous things."

"You're a sensual woman."

"But not a sensible one."

Her words stung. He didn't want her to think of him as a big mistake. He'd been thought of that way, way too often during his life. He didn't want Savannah to feel that way, too. Yet wasn't that really how she should think of him?

"Let's not overanalyze what just happened. Let's just accept it for what it was."

"One last booty call?" she interrupted.

"You were never that," he corrected.

"I was never more than that."

He winced at her conviction. "How can you say that?"

"Because it's true," she insisted.

"I've told you repeatedly that I enjoyed what we shared." He sighed, knowing this wasn't an argument he could win. It wasn't even one he should try to win. "Let's not talk. I'll be gone tomorrow so just let me hold you for a few minutes now."

Her eyes closed. "Fine."

He held her, tracing his fingertips over the lines of her spine, noting how her bones protruded. "Have you lost weight?"

"I thought we weren't going to talk."

"Promise me you'll eat."

"I do eat."

Something in the way she said it made him stare at her. "You've been sick again?"

"I'm fine."

"Apparently not if you're losing weight."

"I've not lost weight and I'm not sick." She sat up and tugged on the sheet, trying to cover her body.

That was when he noticed what he had been too distracted to notice. He studied her lower abdomen. It was only the slightest change, almost imperceptible, even on close inspection. Almost. He glanced up at her, denial and a thousand questions running through his mind.

Oh, God. He knew. Charlie knew she was pregnant.

They'd just had one-last-time-before-he-left sex and he'd noticed her beginning of a pregnancy bump. Savannah hadn't thought about that when she'd thrown herself at him. All she'd been thinking was how good being in his arms had felt.

But her little three-month-along belly stuck out just enough that he'd noticed the subtle change.

"Savannah?"

She tugged the covers further over her body, realized it wasn't near enough. She got up and put on her yoga pants and T-shirt.

"Tell me I'm not seeing what I think I saw."

"You didn't see what you think you saw," she responded as emotionless as she could.

"Yes, I did." The words came out as if they'd escaped from a mangled throat.

"Then don't ask me to tell you that you didn't."

"Explain yourself."

"What do you mean, explain myself? I'd say it's pretty self-explanatory and I didn't get this way by myself so don't go giving me that big bad doctor tone."

"It's true?" He sounded incredulous, and not in a good way. More like he was about to be sick or run away.

He was about to run away.

Drive away, at any rate.

She shrugged. "It doesn't matter."

"You're pregnant? That sure as hell matters to me. How long have you known?"

Savannah winced, guilt slamming her. "A while."

"How long?"

"You remember my good news that I never got to tell you?"

His face was pale, almost ashen. "Since then? Two months and you couldn't find a moment to tell me?"

"I tried." She shrugged as if it were no big deal even though she knew better. "It never felt right. You were leaving. I was staying."

His jaw dropped, worked back and forth. "You weren't going to tell me?"

"I was going to tell you. I just hadn't figured out when."

"When our kid started school? When he hit puberty? Left for college? When?"

She flinched. "Before then. Way before then. Before he's born, but I don't know exactly when I would have told you. Not until after you were moved and settled, I think."

"He? It's a boy?"

He'd zeroed in on the pronoun, but she shrugged. "I don't know. I go for my first ultrasound tomorrow."

"How far along are you?"

"About three months."

His silence spoke volumes long before he looked up and met her gaze. "We always used protection."

She snorted. "Obviously, it wasn't foolproof."

"Obviously. Damn."

Tears stung her eyes. "No, not damn. I don't want anything from you, so don't go damning me or my baby."

"You're pregnant with my child."

Her mouth twisted. "I guess I should be grateful you assume it's yours."

Charlie frowned at Savannah's taunt. Of course he assumed her baby was his. "Who else's would your baby be?"

"I don't know." She hung her head into her hands. "I don't want to fight with you."

Despite how his mind was reeling, how all of him was reeling, remorse at how upset she looked hit him. "We aren't fighting. We are having a discussion about the fact that you are pregnant with my child, have known for two months, and failed to tell me."

"Like you failed to tell me you never planned to stay in Chattanooga? That you had accepted another job?" Although her eyes were red-rimmed, her chin jutted forward defiantly. "Would it have made a difference if I had told you I was pregnant?"

"What do you mean, would it have made a difference? You should have told me."

"What would be different if I had told you two months ago?"

He just stared at her tear-filled eyes and saw his mother. Saw the endless tears, the fights, the heartbreak. Heard the misery of what he'd caused his parents.

He wasn't his father. He'd never be his father. Never.

Only he'd gotten Savannah pregnant.

He wouldn't let Savannah be his mother. He wouldn't do that to her.

He couldn't.

"I'd like to think a lot of things would be different."

"But not you leaving?"

"No, the fact you are pregnant isn't a reason for me not to leave." If anything, her being pregnant was reason for him to leave, to set her free from the misery that was his legacy.

She nodded. "Finally something we agree on."

Her sarcasm was getting to him. "But we do have a lot of things we should've been talking about for the past two months."

"It's six months before the baby arrives. That's more than enough time for whatever we have to say."

Six months. Savannah would have a baby. He would be a father. Six months. Six months. The two words strummed through him like a jungle beat, picking up in tempo with each beat.

"I can't stay." He wasn't sure if the words were for her or as a reminder to himself. His heart pounded. His hands shook. His mind raced. Six months and Savannah's life would change forever.

Her life had already changed forever.

Just as his mother's life had changed forever when she'd gotten pregnant.

Savannah glared. "I'm not asking you to stay."

Charlie's throat swelled so thick he wasn't sure air could get inside. He'd done this. Had changed her from the happy woman she'd been into this angry, bitter woman.

Like father, like son.

No. He wouldn't be like his father. He wouldn't make Savannah pay for getting pregnant for the rest of her life. He'd do right by her financially, more than right. He'd make up to Savannah all the things he hadn't been able to make up to his mother and he'd not stick around to make her miserable the way his father had. He'd go to Nashville, pursue his career, be a silent father to his child, there if needed, but otherwise someone who was far in the background. Savannah would be a good mother. She'd had great role models. Their baby would be better off without his physical presence.

"I don't know what to say," he began after silence lingered too long between them. "I wasn't expecting this."

She gave him a look that cut to the core. "Don't you get it? You don't have to say or do anything. This is my body and I take responsibility for my baby. You can leave and never look back."

That was what he should do. Walk away and stay

out of their lives completely, other than financially. "I can't do that."

He wasn't sure what he could do, but he knew he wanted to do more than just give Savannah and their baby child support.

"Why not?" she asked, her tone full of accusation. "It's what you planned to do an hour ago."

"This is now."

Her eyes narrowed defiantly. "You can't stay."

He closed his eyes, felt tortured. He'd done to Savannah what his father had done to his mother. Not to the extent that Rupert had abused his mother, but Charlie was well on his way. He should have ended things months ago, long before he and Savannah got so attached. He'd known he should have, had repeatedly planned to tell her he needed space, but he just hadn't been able to step away. Not until the job offer from Nashville came. Then he'd had to face that it was time for him to step out of the picture so both he and Savannah could move on with their lives.

For him, that meant a career bump. For her, he'd thought she'd marry someone who could give her the life she dreamed of and raise a family. She was pregnant. He'd ruined everything for her, stolen her dreams.

His life's legacy. Dream-stealer.

He swallowed, trying to clear the lump in his throat. "I'm as much to blame for your circumstances as you are. It wouldn't be right for you to face this alone."

But, even as he said the words, he acknowledged that she would be alone because he'd be in Nashville, and that was right where he needed to be.

CHAPTER SIX

CHARLIE HAD WANTED her ultrasound information, but hadn't said he'd be at the appointment. Since he'd asked for the details, Savannah kept glancing up from her magazine toward the entrance to the radiology department waiting area every few seconds, thinking he'd show.

He hadn't.

Of course he hadn't.

Today was his last day working at the hospital. There was a going away party for him this afternoon in the break room. Hadn't she purposely chosen to take today off for her ultrasound appointment so she could miss the goodbye Charlie to-do?

She'd said her own goodbye the night before. That was the only excuse she could come up with for why she'd had sex with him. That and the fact her body craved him. Apparently, immensely disliking him didn't make a hill of beans' difference to how her body responded to his.

A pity, really. Maybe goodbye would have been

easier had the sex been horrible. Maybe that was what she'd hoped. If so, no such luck. If anything, he'd brought her even higher than she recalled. Must be pregnancy hormones.

The ultrasound tech poked her head out a doorway and called Savannah's name. She set the magazine she'd been idly glancing through down in the seat next to her, then followed the woman back to the ultrasound room.

The tech gave her instructions to change into the hospital gown, then to lie back on the examination table. When Savannah had changed and was on the table, the woman came back into the room and gave a quick rundown of what to expect.

"Nothing will hurt, but the transvaginal view may be a little uncomfortable. I'll be as gentle as possible."

Savannah nodded.

"The conducing gel may be a little cold. Sorry."

Savannah didn't care. She couldn't take her eyes off the computer monitor as images began to appear. She'd seen ultrasounds during nursing school, had helped in labor and delivery during that rotation, but this was different. This was her baby. At first she wasn't able to distinguish features, but then images became recognizable.

A head. A body. Two arms. Two hands. Fingers. Legs. Toes. With the way the baby was turned she couldn't tell if the gender was a boy or a girl, but it didn't matter, just that she was looking at her baby.

"Is everything all right?" she asked as the woman marked the dimensions of the baby's head, length, and then zoomed in on a rapidly beating little heart.

Savannah's own heart beat like crazy at what she was seeing. That was her precious baby's heart. Love filled her. She'd thought her heart already overflowed with love for this baby, but seeing the image of her child made it all so much more real. She couldn't imagine how her heart was going to hold so much love when she actually got to hold her baby.

A knock sounded on the door and both Savannah and the ultrasound tech turned as the receptionist poked her head in, clearly guarding the door.

"Dr. Keele is here and insists he's supposed to be present for this. Is it okay if I let him in?"

Relief that he'd shown flooding her, for their baby's sake, Savannah nodded and the woman said something to someone behind her.

In seconds Charlie was in the room, his gaze fixed first on her, then the monitor screen.

"Sorry I'm late. I did an ablation on Mrs. Barton

this morning and got held up later than intended." He spoke to her but his eyes were on the screen, studying every detail of the image the woman had zoomed into.

"Is she okay?" Savannah asked, searching his face for some sign of what he thought of their baby.

"Considering her level of heart failure, she's doing great. I hope to get her scheduled for the LVAD next week."

"That's fabulous."

"What's fabulous is that healthy little heart," he said, studying the screen.

"Everything looks good?" she asked him rather than the tech.

"I can't say much as to anything other than the heart, but that's a beauty of a heart. Must take after his mother."

"His?" the tech asked. "Do you want to know the sex of the baby today?"

"Yes," Savannah said at the same time as Charlie said, "No."

He corrected himself. "Whatever Savannah wants is fine."

"Well, normally I wouldn't be able to tell you at twelve weeks, but you're actually closer to fourteen so I can confirm it with more certainty. I can write it down and she can look later if you don't want to know?"

"I…" He hesitated. "That would be fine."

Savannah frowned. He didn't want to know if their baby was a boy or a girl? How could he stand not knowing? How could he not be looking overjoyed at the precious image on the screen?

The ultrasound tech went through pointing out different features on the ultrasound, then printed pictures for both Savannah and a separate one for Charlie.

He held the photo loosely in his hand as if he wasn't quite sure what to do with it.

"Here—" the tech handed her a piece of paper "—I wrote the sex of your baby on this. You can look at it whenever you decide you're ready to know."

"Thank you."

"No, thank you," the tech countered. "I love my job and watching new parents see their baby for the first time."

"Thank you," Savannah told the tech again as the woman popped out the disk and handed it to her.

"This has a video clip and all the photos on it. Enjoy your baby's first pictures."

Her baby's first pictures.

Savannah glanced at the image in her hand and knew she'd never seen anything more precious.

Charlie thought he might pass out.

Which was saying a lot. He stood for hours on end doing intricate heart surgeries and had no issues. Seeing a 3D image of a three-month-old fetus should not have him shaking.

Yet he was.

Because the baby was his responsibility.

What he'd once been to his father.

Only when he glanced at the photo he couldn't find the hatred his father had felt. Nor the resentment his mother had felt. He couldn't find anything except a deep ache inside.

He was going to be a father.

He'd gotten Savannah pregnant.

He was leaving this evening to move two hours away. Savannah and his baby would be here, in Chattanooga.

That was for the best.

He'd lived the other option and it had been hell.

But seeing his baby, seeing Savannah's excitement at every image, got to him, because that was something he didn't have, would never have.

Something he couldn't let himself have because

he couldn't risk doing to her what his father had done to their family.

Maybe his father had even felt torn at the beginning, had thought he was doing the right thing when he'd married Charlie's mother. Maybe they'd been happy to begin with. Maybe.

All Charlie could recall were the fights and the tears.

The bitterness and resentment.

The agony that had been his mother's life.

The misery that had been his life, his father's life.

The tragic end to his mother's life.

His teeth clenched. He wanted no part of it.

Not for Savannah.

Not for their baby.

Not for himself.

He didn't want to be like his father, didn't want Savannah to be like his mother. He glanced at the photo he held. He wanted better for his baby than what he'd had.

The sudden need to do something overwhelmed him.

"Thank you for this," he told the tech. He nodded to Savannah without meeting her eyes, then left the room.

He heard Savannah apologize to the tech for

his abrupt behavior, explaining he had to get back to work.

A memory from the past slammed into him.

A memory of his mother making excuses for his father's abrupt behavior. To him. To neighbors. To his school teachers.

Funny, he'd forgotten that during his younger days his mother would try to explain away his father's lack of affection, explain away why he was gone more than he was home. Before the end she'd quit making excuses. For his father and for herself.

Now, Savannah was pregnant and making excuses for him.

Already it had started.

He was following in his father's footsteps whether he wanted to or not.

Which was why he folded up the photo and slid it into his pocket. He couldn't look at it anymore. He couldn't be involved because that life in Savannah's belly would be a helluva lot better off without Charlie in it.

That much he knew.

He'd set up some type of trust for the baby, for Savannah, to help with financial needs, and he'd stay away.

Maybe Nashville wasn't far enough to keep him away from what he was leaving in Chattanooga.

The only thing strong enough to keep him away was the past.

"He left, knowing you were pregnant? I mean, I know he left last month," Chrissie corrected herself, waving her spoon around as she talked. "But he knew you were pregnant and he still left?" Her friend shook her head in disbelief. "How could he do that? I didn't understand before and I sure don't now that I know he knows you are pregnant."

They sat at the small four-person dining room table and kept their voices low as Joss was curled up asleep on the sofa.

Savannah shrugged. "I didn't want him to stay. Not because I'm pregnant. Not at all. Not anymore."

Savannah forced herself to take a bite of the vegetable beef stew she'd put in her crock pot that morning, prior to leaving for her twelve-hour shift. The stew might have been the best thing she'd ever stuck in her mouth. Savannah wouldn't know. Nothing had much taste these days, but at least most of her "morning" sickness had passed and she'd eat fairly healthy for a few nights on the stew. Chrissie had jumped at the chance to sit and talk with Savannah as, for the most part, Savannah had shut her friends and family out for the last month. She'd moped around long enough, and had decided it was time to get back to living life, back to feeling like herself. She was strong. She didn't need a man. She had this.

She'd invited her friend over to eat and have a girls' powwow. She'd told Chrissie earlier in the month that she was pregnant, had told everyone at work earlier that day. She hadn't necessarily been ready to face the knowing eyes of her coworkers, but she'd caught more than one coworker staring at her midsection as if trying to decide if she was or wasn't, despite her attempts at hiding her pregnancy beneath her scrubs. The first three months had been easy to conceal her barely-there belly. But, over the past month, her tummy had blossomed.

Other than a few expressions of, "Oh, honey!", everyone had been supportive. Even the *Oh, honey!s* had hugged her and said they'd help any way they could. She'd faked a big smile and told everyone how happy she was at the prospect of being a mother.

She shouldn't have had to fake that smile.

She was happy about being a mother. At times,

she was over the moon at the thought of being a mother. At others, she wanted to crawl into the fetal position and cry.

Darn Charlie for stealing her joy.

Darn her for allowing him to steal her joy.

Darn him for leaving her.

Darn her for caring.

"We're better off without him." She rubbed her stomach, and felt the tiny movements she'd been feeling for the past few days. At first she hadn't been positive if the tiny flutters were the baby or her body. Now, there was no doubt when she felt the little movements. Her baby was growing and she should be ecstatic. Instead, the first time she'd been positive of what she'd been feeling, she'd called her mother and described the feelings, described her joy, then burst into tears that she couldn't stop. Thirty minutes later her worried mother had shown up on her doorstep and ended up staying the night. Pathetic.

Not how her mother had raised her. After her father had died, Sally had struggled to make ends meet. She'd been a stay-at-home mom, but Savannah's father hadn't planned on dying so young and hadn't had life insurance. He'd left his family rich in love, but otherwise poor. Determined that Savannah would never be caught in a similar situation, Sally had raised Savannah to think for herself, to be able to take care of herself financially, to be strong and independent.

No doubt she'd disappointed her mother.

"I don't need him." She didn't. She might have had a weak moment or two, but that didn't mean she needed Charlie. She would raise her baby and she'd do a fantastic job.

Leaning back against her dining room chair, Chrissie frowned. "What is wrong with that man? How could he just leave like that? A blind fool could see that he's crazy about you."

Spooning another bite of stew, Savannah shook her head. She'd thought the same thing, once upon a time. She'd gotten over that foolishness. "That was just sex."

Chrissie didn't look convinced. "I sure didn't think that's all it was."

"Welcome to the club." She wrapped her lips around the spoon and slowly pulled it from her mouth, then sighed.

"Now you do?"

"He's gone and I've not heard from him since he left. Of course it's what I think."

Chrissie took a drink of her soda. "I'm not sure

what to tell you, except I've never seen a man more besotted than he was for you."

"Sexual attraction," she reminded.

"Then I envied you sexual attraction, because it was palpable every time he looked at you or said your name. You walked into a room and he couldn't take his eyes off you." Chrissie shook her dark head in denial. "I just can't believe he left you. Especially knowing you're pregnant."

"Believe." Any sliver of hope she'd had had been crushed when he'd walked out of the ultrasound room without a backward glance. Literally and figuratively. He'd been gone a month and she'd not heard from him. Not even a text to say, *Hi, how are you? How's pregnant life?* Nothing.

Because he was gone.

Gone and wanted her to know he was gone for good.

Fine. Let him stay gone. She had her family, her friends, and her precious baby. She'd ended up flushing the folded paper with the baby's gender written on it, deciding that she wanted to wait. The baby's sex didn't matter. Either way, Savannah was going to love this baby so much that it wouldn't matter that his or her dad wasn't there.

She did love this baby that much. More.

"Honestly, since he never planned to stay in Chattanooga, I'm glad he's gone. The longer he stayed the more difficult letting go would have been." Not that she could imagine it having hurt any more than it had, but still.

"Maybe he had to leave for some secret CIA mission or something that he wasn't allowed to tell you."

"Hah," Savannah scoffed at her friend's outlandish suggestion. "Nice try, but let's face it. Charlie was a jerk and, as far as I'm concerned, good riddance."

A knock on her apartment door had both women looking at each other and Savannah scooting back her chair in hopes the noise didn't disturb Joss.

"You expecting someone?"

"No." She wasn't. She glanced through the peephole and saw a fiftyish-looking man in a business suit carrying a large legal-sized manila envelope.

"Fancy-looking salesman," she muttered to her friend, then called, "Who is it?" through the doorway.

"Kinda late for a salesman," Chrissie muttered from where she still sat at the dining table.

"George Peterson," the man answered. "I'm here on behalf of Dr. Charlie Keele."

On behalf of? Had something happened to Charlie?

Without another thought, she undid her safety chain and flung the door open. "Is Charlie okay?"

The man looked startled at her question. "He's fine."

She sighed in relief, tension letting loose of her neck and shoulders. "Then who are you and why are you here?"

He held out the envelope. "I'm an attorney. Dr. Keele hired me to conduct some business transactions for him and to personally deliver this to you. Everything has been recorded at the court house and this is your copy."

"My copy?" She knew she probably sounded crazy, but she had no clue what he was talking about. What had been recorded at the court house?

Then it hit her.

A lawyer representing Charlie.

Legal-sized papers recorded at the court house.

Her heart squeezed so tightly it skipped a beat.

Charlie was going for custody.

She gritted her teeth together, then shook her head. "I don't want those."

The lawyer looked even more startled. "Dr. Keele has been very generous."

"I'm sure he has," she spat out, placing a protective hand over her belly. "But you can tell him to kiss my—"

"Ma'am, I think you should—"

This time she cut him off. "And I think you should go. You're not welcome. You can tell Dr. Keele he's not, either."

The lawyer looked torn a moment, then shoved the envelope toward her and left before she could toss it back.

"I'll fight him on this," she called out to the retreating man, who glanced at her over his shoulder, a confused frown on his face.

"What was all that about?" Chrissie asked, walking up next to her and staring down the hallway.

"Charlie is filing for custody."

Chrissie's mouth dropped open. "Seriously? I thought he didn't want anything to do with the baby?"

"Obviously I was wrong about that, too." She waved the envelope in front of her friend. "He can't have my baby."

Okay, so logically she knew he could, and would, have time with their baby. That was what she wanted, right? For her baby to grow up with a loving father to be there for him or her, even if he hadn't been able to be there for Savannah? She did want that, but the thought of him taking her to court... Her stew threatened to make a reappearance.

How dare he do this to her so coldly? Without even discussing it with her first? They'd been together a year. A year! Didn't she deserve an actual pick-up of the phone and, *Hey, I've decided I do want to be a part of my child's life. Let's talk about it?* How could she have thought she knew him so well, inside and out, and have been so very wrong?

She'd thought he loved her. Lust and love were two very different things. Because she'd wanted to believe she'd credited Charlie for being more than he was. He was nothing better than every other Joe Schmoe looking for a good time.

Yet even now she had a difficult time convincing herself of that. Look at what a great con job he'd pulled on her that, even after a month of not hearing from him, she still struggled to believe that he wasn't the awesome man she'd put up on a pedestal. After he'd proved that she didn't matter enough to discuss major life decisions with, such as moving two hours away or wanting legal rights over their child.

"Maybe he just wants visitation," Chrissie suggested, staring at Savannah. "If so, that's a good thing, right?"

It was. Although anxiety coursed through her, she truly did want Charlie to be a part of their baby's life. Yes, that made things a hundred times worse for her because it would mean seeing him, but their baby knowing his or her father was more important.

If Charlie wanted reasonable legal rights to their child, she wouldn't fight him despite what she'd flung at the retreating lawyer.

She threw the oversized envelope down on the dining room table next to her half-eaten bowl of stew and slowly sank onto a chair. Chrissie joined her and took her hand into hers, holding her tightly. They sat in silence for a couple of minutes before Chrissie nudged her.

"Maybe you should open the envelope to see what it says."

Savannah closed her eyes and tried to go back to the happy place where she'd existed just a few months ago when she'd thought she was the luckiest woman alive. She'd been so naïve, so trusting, so caught up in being in love that she'd just looked at Charlie through rose-colored glasses and seen what she wanted to see. Foolish. Never again would she be so easily fooled. Never again would she open up and give her heart away.

She didn't need him.

She didn't need anyone.

"Savannah? How can you not rip that open?"

Resting her head in her hands, she sighed. "I don't want to know what it says."

"Well, I do." Chrissie picked up the envelope as if to open it. "If you're not going to open this, I am."

"Give it to me." Savannah took the envelope from her friend and tore into the end. Nausea rose from the pit of her stomach. Her baby's future had been reduced to legal documents compiled by a lawyer.

She pulled out the blue-backed document and a key, stared at it in confusion, read the lawyer's letter in even further confusion.

In total shock, she lifted her gaze to her curious friend. "He's lost his mind."

Chrissie gave her an expectant look. "Well, what did he ask for? Surely not full custody. And what's up with the key?"

Words failed her so, with unsteady hands, she gave the papers to her friend and closed her shaky fingers around the key, letting the metal dig into her palm. She welcomed the discomfort, hoping it pulled her back to reality.

Chrissie's eyes widened. "Savannah! Oh, my!"

She nodded. Exactly.

"He's given you his house. Savannah, this is unbelievable. He deeded you his house!"

CHAPTER SEVEN

HE MIGHT NOT be home, Savannah told herself for the hundredth time since she'd taken off toward Nashville. It was a Thursday morning. He was probably working. Or he could be out of town. Or it could be his day off work and he could be out with someone.

That made her pause.

It had been a month. Had he moved on? Started dating someone else? When she showed up at his house, would he have another woman there?

Had deeding his house to her made him feel absolved from his obligations to her and their child?

Ha, she was going to give him a piece of her mind over his high-handedness. She didn't want his house or his money or anything material from him.

She didn't want anything from him, period. Not anymore.

She was on her way to tell him that and to throw his deed and key in his handsome face. He couldn't just do something like that. It wasn't okay and a big gift, a huge gift, didn't make it okay that he'd walked away from their child.

She was going to tell him that. And more. And… she didn't know what, exactly. Just that since the night before she'd been burning inside, had woken with that burn still present and, before she'd made a conscious decision, she'd been on her way to Nashville rather than the grocery store, as she'd originally set out to.

He would likely be at work, so she'd go there first. But, if not, she knew right where Charlie's apartment was. Sure, the weather had been better two months ago when she'd gone with him to Nashville than the cold drizzly rain that was falling today, but that was okay. The weather matched her mood.

No, if the weather matched her mood the wind would be howling and the sky would be blood-red, not a dreary gray.

She clung to her anger. Anger was better than sadness and loss. She'd experienced enough of that over the past few months. No more.

How dare he?

That was the question she asked herself over and over as she headed north on I-24 toward Nashville.

Just inside the city limits, the traffic slowed to a sudden stop in all four lanes.

Savannah's heart thudded like crazy as she applied her brakes, hoping they didn't lock, hoping she'd keep from slamming into the large black vehicle in front of her.

The next few seconds drew out in slow motion, with her heartbeat doing overtime. Her sweat glands too as her skin was drenched with clammy stickiness. Despite the rain-slick road, she somehow got her sedan stopped just inches before crashing into the sports utility vehicle in front of her.

Heart pounding, she let out the breath she hadn't realized she'd been holding.

In the next second she cried out as the impact from whatever had been behind her crashed into her with great force, ramming her car into the SUV.

Her body jerked forward against her seatbelt, digging painfully into her chest and shoulder. What breath she had remaining inside her gushed out in a hard whoosh. Her neck snapped forward, then whipped back. The sound of metal crunching into metal deafened her ears.

The second she thought it was over, another impact hit as another vehicle failed to stop in time. She jerked forward and back again, this time not as hard as the previous, but pain ripped through her body all the same.

Tensing, she prepared herself for yet another hit and another as no doubt more cars would join into the interstate pile-up, but none came. Just the sound of the rain still falling around her and nothing more.

Trying not to panic, she began to take stock of the damage. To her and to her car.

She hurt. Her neck. Her shoulder. Her belly. She took a tentative breath. Pain shock-waved through her. Not good.

She wiggled her fingers and her toes. Everything seemed to be moving as it should. Maybe. Odd, but she really wasn't sure if she'd moved at all. She tried to raise her arm, but doing so hurt too much so she quit trying. She must have bit her tongue or the inside of her cheek as the strong metallic taste of blood filled her senses. Or maybe it was her nose, she thought as a drop of blood fell from her nostril. Despite the pain, she wiped at her face, registered the red liquid on her hand. She wasn't sure why her nose was bleeding as she'd had her seatbelt on, but it definitely was.

Or maybe the blood came from somewhere else

on her face? She wasn't sure. Did it even matter where the blood was coming from?

That there was warm liquid between her legs, she also registered.

No, she thought. No. No. *No*.

"Ma'am, are you all right?" a man who appeared to be in his early twenties asked from outside her shattered driver's door window. She glanced at her busted windshield, at the shattered passenger door window, at the SUV that was where the front of her car should be.

She glanced down, realized her steering wheel was against her chest, that she couldn't see the lower half of her body.

"Ma'am?"

She turned back toward the driver's window, opened her mouth to tell the young man that no, she wasn't okay, that she couldn't feel her baby moving, and to please do something, but nothing came out. She was still trying to tell him as her eyes became too heavy to stay open.

So she closed them.

Charlie made his way toward the heart failure unit at Vanderbilt University Medical Center. He'd consulted on a patient that morning prior to heading over to teach a class to second year medical students, and wanted to pop his head back in to check on the woman before seeing his scheduled afternoon patients.

His stomach rumbled as he passed a food cart.

The food didn't smell that appetizing, but his stomach was lodging its protest that he had once again forgotten to eat lunch.

Had he eaten breakfast?

He honestly couldn't remember. Every day ran into the next and they all seemed the same. They all seemed lackluster. They all seemed to be missing something.

Maybe it was him missing something.

Or, more accurately, missing someone.

Savannah.

His throat tightened just at her name consciously passing through his mind.

He'd not talked to her. Not a single time. He'd decided staying away altogether was best.

He'd thought about her, though. A lot. Almost all the time.

He also thought of their baby, despite doing his best not to think of the life he and Savannah had created. How could he think of anything else?

He was going to be a father.

He knew nothing of being a good father. Nothing.

That Savannah would be a good mother wasn't even in doubt. She would be an excellent mother, just as her mother had been. In that respect, their child had hit the parenting jackpot. Savannah would do everything she could to give their child a good life.

As would he.

After her ultrasound, he'd contacted his realtor, told her he wanted to pull the house off the market, then he'd had his lawyer take care of everything else.

Savannah and their child would have a nice home in a good neighborhood. She wouldn't have to worry about providing a roof over her and their baby's head. She wouldn't have to worry about anything financially. He'd see to that. If she wanted to stay home and raise their child, she'd be able to.

It was the least he could do since he couldn't be with her.

Guilt hit him.

Guilt he shouldn't be feeling. He was taking care of her. In a much better way than if he was physically there because he wouldn't be making her miserable, making their child miserable. He wouldn't be standing in the way of her happiness.

He was doing for her what his father should have done for his mother. He was letting her be free so she could live her life without being encumbered with a man who would eventually resent her presence and destroy who she was. Not to mention the damage he could do to a child's mental and emotional stability.

Currently, it was difficult to imagine that because he craved Savannah's presence so intensely he dreamed of her every time his eyes closed. He'd see someone with red hair and be struck with the memory of the first time he'd unclipped Savannah's hair, the way her long tresses had tumbled over her shoulders, how silky the strands had felt between his fingers as he'd kissed her throat, her neck, her creamy shoulders.

He missed her.

But his father's voice echoing through his head couldn't be silenced. Nor could the memory of his mother and her tragic death.

Savannah was better off without him.

Much better off.

No matter how much he missed her, he'd stay away.

He checked on his patient, made chart notes for one of the residents to follow up on, and left the unit. He'd gotten to the elevator and pushed the down arrow when his cell phone rang.

He glanced at the number. It wasn't one he recognized.

He started to ignore it as he'd soon be stepping into the elevator and would likely lose the signal anyway, but some inner force had him sliding his finger across the screen.

"Charlie Keele?"

Charlie didn't recognize the male voice. "Yes?"

"This is Sergeant Oliver Casteel. I'm with the Metro Police Department."

The elevator dinged and the door slid open, revealing an elderly couple and a nurse inside the car already. Brow furrowed to form a tight knot between his eyes, Charlie motioned for the elevator to go on without him and stepped away from the doors. He couldn't fathom why the police would be calling him, but he sure didn't want to step into the elevator and possibly lose the signal.

"You were listed as the emergency contact for Savannah Carter."

Listed as the emergency contact.

Charlie's knees threatened to buckle. There were very few reasons why the Police Department made phone calls.

"She's been in an accident."

"Is she…" His voice broke and he couldn't finish his question. He was used to dealing with life and death, with emergencies. Yet nothing had prepared him for this phone call and the very real fear gripping him. Savannah had been in an accident and the police were calling him.

"She's been in a multi-car accident. She's alive but seriously injured."

She was alive.

"I'm calling because she had you listed as her emergency contact," the officer continued.

His brain raced. "I'll let her mother know and head to Chattanooga immediately."

"Chattanooga?"

What the officer had said registered. "She's in Nashville?"

"She's been airlifted to Vanderbilt University Medical Center."

Airlifted. Vanderbilt. Savannah was there.

"I'm there. Here." Savannah was here. "I work there. Here." He wasn't making much sense, had no idea what else he said to the officer, knew that he responded to the man's comments about Savannah's personal belongings and her car being totaled and towed to a local garage, but all he really focused on was getting to the emergency department. Today, the hospital seemed a hundred times larger than he knew the building to be.

He had to flash his name badge a few times but, fortunately, once in the emergency department, it didn't take long to find her. The helicopter had obviously just landed and she'd only been inside the hospital a few minutes. She was surrounded by nurses and at least two emergency room physicians. A portable X-ray machine was being rolled up to no doubt check for internal injuries.

"She's pregnant, just over four months," he said to no one in particular. At this point, he had no idea if she'd lost the baby. He just knew pregnant women didn't get X-rays unless it was an emergency.

Blood streaked Savannah's face. Wires and tubes jutted out from everywhere. She lay on the gurney quite lifeless other than the soft moaning of pain that the hustle-bustle and machines couldn't quite drown out.

This was an emergency.

Oh, God, please let her be okay.

Please let their baby be okay.

He tried to objectively assess what he could see

of Savannah. Tried and failed. He had no objectivity where she was concerned.

His eyes took in her pale appearance, her blood-streaked face, her lack of movement, her legs that had been elevated as if to prevent shock. Had she lost that much blood?

"Can I help you?" one of the nurses asked, glancing up from where she punched data into an infusion pump.

"Is she…?"

What was he asking? Of course she was still alive. The monitors showed a heartbeat, sounded a reassuring beep. Then there were the painful moans. But Savannah wasn't awake. There was too much activity around her. Intravenous lines rapidly putting fluid into her body and even a pint of blood being infused as fast as her veins would take it.

"You are?" the nurse asked, eyeing him as if she was going to call Security any moment.

What could he say? He was nothing to Savannah. Not anymore.

"She's pregnant with my baby."

Was she still pregnant with their baby? Had the wreck robbed her of their child?

The emergency room doctor and nurse exchanged

looks, then the nurse who'd been talking to him stepped away from Savannah, glanced closer at Charlie's name badge. "I'm sorry, Dr. Keele, but I'm going to have to ask you to step out. We've got to get her into surgery STAT. One of the doctors or myself will come find you as quickly as possible and let you know what's going on."

With that, another nurse escorted him out of the cubicle and to a waiting area, where he waited. And waited.

Charlie had no idea how much time had passed. He'd had the presence of mind to call one of the residents and have her see his scheduled afternoon patients but, other than that, he wasn't sure he'd had a rational thought for hours.

What his thoughts had been was irrational. He'd wanted to pull rank, to barge into wherever Savannah was and demand to know exactly what was going on. To do that might slow down her care, might waste vital time being spent on him rather than her.

So he sat.

He thought of breaking hospital policy and logging into Savannah's medical chart and finding out what was happening. He could be fired for doing so. Yet the thought was tempting.

Surgery? What kind of surgery? What about the baby? Did Savannah have internal injuries? God, he wished he knew something—that he knew she was going to be okay.

If he didn't hear something soon, maybe he'd use his badge to at least get someone on the emergency room staff to tell him something because the waiting was killing him.

Savannah's mother wasn't faring much better. Other than asking if he knew anything when she'd first arrived, she'd not said much to him. Savannah's cousin had driven her mother and her aunt the two-hour trip and the three of them sat praying while he paced back and forth across the room. No doubt she hated him. No doubt she should. He'd gotten her daughter pregnant and walked away. Despite his knowing that was best for Savannah and their baby, to an outsider that made him look like the bad guy. That was okay. He knew in the long run his not being in Savannah's life would be more beneficial to her and their child than living the hell that had been his and his mother's life.

Just when he thought he couldn't stand anymore, the nurse entered the room and motioned to follow her. He motioned to Savannah's family and they went with him. Without really telling him anything, the nurse put them in a consult room.

Within a couple of minutes of being shown the room, a vascular surgeon he vaguely recognized entered the room.

A vascular surgeon.

Why had Savannah needed a vascular surgeon? He'd been expecting an orthopedic or an internist or a hospitalist or an obstetrician, but not a vascular surgeon. Maybe, with as much blood as Savannah had apparently lost, he should have.

"How is my daughter?" Savannah's mother asked. The surgeon didn't directly respond, just made brief eye contact with the older women and Savannah's cousin, then turned to Charlie.

He rose to his feet and shook the man's hand.

"Hello, Dr. Keele. I'm Dr. Trenton. I hear you've recently joined our heart failure team. My nurse says you're acquainted with Miss Carter and were her emergency contact."

Savannah's mother didn't look happy at having her question ignored, that he'd been who the police officer had called, and, honestly, Charlie didn't blame her.

He didn't recall telling the nurse much of anything about himself, other than he was Savannah's baby's father, but maybe he had said more. Or maybe she'd done some research. She'd seen his name tag. A simple Internet search would have told her that much and more. As far as being acquainted with Savannah, he wasn't sure how to label himself so he just nodded and asked Savannah's mother's question. "How is she?"

"Lucky to be alive and in recovery. Barring something unforeseen, I believe she's out of the woods now that her bleed has been repaired. She was pretty banged up. Mostly deep bruising, as far as we can tell, except her peroneal artery was lacerated in her left leg. We're not exactly sure what cut her, just that she had a significant puncture laceration. Fortunately, one of the accident witnesses was a firefighter and he got her free from the car, made a pressure bandage for her leg, and kept her legs elevated. He saved her life, but she still lost quite a bit of blood."

"But she is going to be okay?" Had Charlie asked or her mother? He didn't know. It didn't matter. All that mattered was that Savannah was going to be all right.

Dr. Trenton nodded. "I have every reason to believe she is going to be fine. The surgical repair of the artery was a success. She's off the ventilator the helicopter team put in to maintain an airway in case of internal injuries and she's breathing just fine on her own. As far as we can tell, there aren't any broken bones. I don't expect any surgical complications. We'll monitor her for a few days, just to be sure and to make sure there aren't any unforeseen internal injuries."

Charlie let that register, then asked what no one had mentioned, not even Savannah's family. "The baby?"

The man met his gaze and gave him a somber look. "She hasn't miscarried yet, but her body did sustain major trauma. Certainly, the baby is at risk."

"She's going to lose our baby?"

The surgeon sighed. "I wish I could tell you a definite no but, with the trauma to her body, a miscarriage is a real possibility. She had a few contractions earlier but they seem to have stopped now that her blood volume levels are normalized. A high risk obstetrician has been assigned to the case and will be overseeing her care once she's transferred out of recovery. No doubt she'll be able to give you much more information than what I know. What I can tell you is that Miss Carter's ultrasound has showed the placenta is intact and, best we can tell, there aren't any leaks. The baby's heartbeat has remained strong and steady, but again, Miss Carter lost a lot of blood and had to have several pints infused. The neonatal unit is aware and on standby if she or the baby gets in distress. A team of doctors will be monitoring them both closely."

Even with the hospital's excellent neonatology unit, their baby wouldn't survive at such an early stage of pregnancy. Savannah was only four months pregnant. Definitely, the hospital was equipped to handle early deliveries and had many successful cases of survival, but four months was too early. Way too early.

Charlie's eyes prickled with moisture and he sank to one of the vinyl-covered chairs in the small waiting area.

"Thank God Savannah's going to be all right," her mother said, not commenting on the baby. "When can we see her?"

The surgeon nodded at her mother, then said, "It'll be another fifteen or twenty minutes before she'll be released from recovery, then she'll be transferred to the high risk obstetric unit." He met Charlie's gaze. "Normally, you wouldn't be able to see her until she was transferred onto the floor but, as a courtesy, Dr. Keele can see her before she's transferred."

Savannah's mother grumbled, but didn't say anything beyond.

Charlie closed his eyes. He would like to see Savannah.

Question was, would Savannah want him there?

If she didn't, could he really blame her?

CHAPTER EIGHT

SAVANNAH HURT.

All over.

And inside.

She hurt there, too.

"Take a deep breath," someone told her. The voice was kind, gentle, comforting almost, and sounded so far away.

"Savannah, you need to take a deep breath."

The voice wasn't as soft this time. There was more urgency to the tone. A beeping was sounding in the background that didn't quite fit in Savannah's fuzzy mind.

A deep breath. She could do that. She pulled air into her lungs then stopped at the excruciating pain.

Maybe she couldn't do that.

Why did it hurt to breathe?

"I know it hurts," the voice empathized. "But you need to take some deep breaths and get your oxygen saturation higher. Dr. Trenton isn't going to release you to be transferred to your room until you're stable. Breathe."

Transferred to her room.

Despite how heavy her eyelids felt, Savannah pried her lids apart. Fluorescent lights shone in her eyes and she quickly closed her lids to block out the brightness.

She was in a hospital. That much registered.

"Blue," the voice that had told her to breathe said. "With that red hair, I wondered if they would be. Your eyes, that is."

Savannah exerted great effort and ordered her eyes to open again. Slowly, they obeyed and she struggled to focus on her surroundings.

"I was hoping you'd open them on your own before I had to do your next neuro check."

A bright room with artificial lighting. So bright it made holding her eyes open even more of a challenge. Or maybe it was the fact that they felt so puffy, almost swollen shut, that made it so difficult to keep her lids pried apart. Even the slightest movement sent new shockwaves of pain through her body.

"Take another big breath to keep your oxygen saturation up," the nurse repeated. "Your baby needs you taking big breaths."

Her baby. Oh, no. Had she? No, the woman had told her to breathe deeply to get her O2 sats up for her baby. If she'd miscarried, her breathing wouldn't affect her baby.

Her baby was alive.

Still, she wanted reassurance, especially as she didn't feel any movement. Not that she always did, just that currently she felt nothing.

Nothing except pain. Great pain.

"My baby? Did I…?"

"Your baby is still holding his or her own. See." The woman gestured toward a monitor.

Savannah squinted toward the direction the woman gestured. There were a lot of monitors and medical equipment hooked to her, two of which displayed steady heartbeats, one much more rapid than the other. One hundred and forty-eight beats per minute. Her baby had a good, steady fetal heartbeat.

She was in a hospital. Her baby was alive. She was alive. Why was she in a hospital? Why did she hurt so much?

"What happened?"

"You don't remember?" the nurse asked.

She closed her eyes and strained to recall. Horror joined her pain. "I was in a wreck. My car was hit and then I hit the car in front of me and was trapped between them."

"From what I was told, that sounds right," the nurse agreed. "There was a fender bender that put traffic at a sudden stop on the interstate. Apparently, you were able to get stopped, but the driver behind you wasn't paying attention and never braked. One of the witnesses said the driver was texting while driving." The nurse gave a disgusted look. "You were slammed into by that car and that smashed you into the car in front of you. Then, another car hit the car that hit you and crushed you in between the two vehicles even more. I'm not a hundred percent that's accurate, but it's what I was told. Regardless, you are lucky to still be with us."

Savannah relived the impact followed by another impact. She remembered thinking the hits, the being jerked forward, was never going to end, that she was going to die in her car.

"Was anyone else hurt?" she asked, almost afraid of the answer. When in nursing school, she'd done a few rotations where she'd worked the emergency department, worked motor vehicle accidents. She knew how serious they could be.

The nurse winced and Savannah knew someone

had been injured. By the nurse's expression, seriously injured.

"The driver who hit you, the one texting while driving, died instantly."

Savannah's heart squeezed. That impact that had jarred her very being, someone had died in that instant.

She could have died.

Her baby could have died.

Her gaze went to the fetal heart monitor, taking in the rapid little heartbeats.

She might hurt all over, but at least her baby was alive.

"Sad." Her throat felt so dry, almost swelled shut.

The nurse seemed to read her mind and offered a sip. "Just a little one to begin with, though, until we see how you do."

Savannah was grateful for something wet. The nurse held the cup to where she could take a sip through the straw. She'd barely gotten a few drops in her mouth when the nurse pulled back the cup. "Sorry. Just a little for now. I'll give you more in a few minutes if you do okay with that."

She wanted more, but her nurse's brain understood the reasons why. Not that she felt her brain was working correctly. She didn't. A fog clouded her mind, making thinking a conscious effort rather than something that came naturally.

Just how hurt was she?

Her left leg felt crazy heavy, much more so than her arms and right leg, which also seemed to be made of lead. Pain racked her body and yet pinpointing where she hurt, or even where she hurt most, seemed impossible. Quite simply, every inch of her hurt. She was sure it did.

When she hurt so completely, when the wreck had been as bad as she was realizing it was, how could her baby have survived?

"I can see my baby's heart beating, but you're sure he or she is okay? That nothing happened during the wreck?"

"You've had several tests. Your ultrasound didn't show any abnormalities. It seems your body absorbed most of the impact of the wreck and protected your baby."

Hopefully. She wanted to protect her baby, to always keep her baby safe from harm. She'd slept through an ultrasound where she could have seen her beautiful baby? That was sad.

"Did they take pictures?"

The nurse's brows rose. "Pardon?"

"During my ultrasound, did they take pictures of my baby?"

Smiling gently, the nurse shook her head. "Not that I'm aware of, but I've no doubt you'll be having another ultrasound prior to leaving the hospital. Probably a few more. You can ask the sonographer to print you a photo at that time."

Savannah went to nod, but her head didn't co-operate.

Panic must have shown in her eyes because the nurse touched her arm.

"You're in a neck stabilization brace. You got whipped around hard. The hospitalist overseeing your care wants you left in the brace for now to keep your neck stable. Nothing's broken," she assured her. "The doctor is just being cautious."

What had the wreck done to her body? All she'd asked about was the baby.

"What is wrong with me?"

"Mostly severe bruising, multiple lacerations, a few of which required stitching, and then you had a puncture wound on your leg that tore the peroneal artery. That's why your left leg may feel really heavy. One of the vascular surgeons repaired the bleed."

An arterial bleed.

"I checked your wound before you woke up. He did a great job. Once it's healed, you'll only have a tiny scar."

At this point the size of a scar seemed such a trivial matter.

Just so long as her baby was going to be okay, everything else was trivial. The fog that clouded her mind moved in thicker, darker.

Exhausted, she closed her eyes. When she next opened them, the nurse was standing over her, telling her to breathe deeply again.

The last time she'd breathed deeply, she'd hurt. Vaguely she recalled talking to the nurse. She couldn't recall if they'd just had the conversation or if it had been hours ago.

She already hurt. She sure didn't want to do anything that made that pain worse.

But she had her baby to think about.

She took a few deep breaths and reminded herself that the intense pain was worth it if it helped the baby.

"Good job," the nurse praised.

Charlie wasn't supposed to be on this side of medicine. He just wasn't. He'd been there, done that with his grandfather. His mother had died instantly in her car wreck and his father had been ill for a while but, stubbornly, had died in his sleep at home rather than at a hospital where he could have received medical care. Only with his grandfather had Charlie sat at the hospital. He'd felt so helpless then.

He felt so helpless now.

Even more so as the nurse led him through to the recovery room where Savannah lay on the hospital bed. The scene that met him had his knees threatening to buckle.

Her face had multiple bruises and lacerations. Her left upper and lower eyelids were a purplish blue and significantly swollen. Her lower lip was swollen and busted in the middle. Her neck was in a stabilization brace. Her left leg was propped up on a pillow and covered with the white blanket that was tucked around her.

"This is Dr. Keele. He works in cardiology," the nurse introduced him to the recovery room nurse who was hovering over Savannah.

The recovery nurse gave Charlie's escort an odd look, one that clearly asked why he was there.

"I'm a friend of your patient," he explained, realizing the woman wondered why the nurse was bringing a cardiologist to see her post-op vascular patient.

At his voice, Savannah's eyes opened, her left only partially parting beneath her swollen lids. Her eye was bloodshot where capillaries had burst and bled, trapping the blood.

She didn't speak, just touched her tongue to her lips as if to moisten them. The recovery room nurse, in tune with her patient, dabbed Savannah's lips with a moist swab.

"There. That should help."

Savannah moved slightly, as if trying to nod, then let out a soft moan.

"Don't try moving right now other than to take some big, deep breaths," the nurse instructed. "I'm going to step over here for a few minutes to give you a bit of privacy." Her gaze met Charlie's. "Make sure she keeps breathing deep."

Charlie wasn't sure he wanted to be left alone with Savannah. Then again, having the nurse observe their conversation couldn't be a good thing either. Who knew what Savannah was going to say to him? She'd probably tell him to go to hell.

The past few hours, he'd felt as if that was where he'd been.

What did it matter what she said? She was alive, could say whatever she wanted, and he'd just be thankful that she had the ability to speak.

He stepped next to the hospital bed, placed his hand over hers, grateful for the warmth he felt there, for the lifeblood still flowing through her body.

"Dr. Trenton says you're going to be okay," he said, his thumb rubbing over her hand and his voice choking up. Should he touch her? How could he not? He wanted to pull her into his arms and hold her close and protect her from the whole world.

As if he could protect her.

He couldn't. Just as he'd not been able to protect his mother. She'd died and it had been his fault.

He stood next to Savannah's hospital bed, caressing her hand and wishing he knew what to say to make everything better.

Wishing he could take away her pain.

She stared at him from between her swollen eyelids that looked as if they were getting heavier and heavier. Her oxygen saturation alarm sounded, indicating that her level had dropped and earning them a concerned glance from the nurse.

"Take a deep breath, Savannah. You've got to breathe deep to keep your sats up."

"Don't tell me what to do," she mumbled, but took several deep breaths after doing so.

"I just want you to be okay."

"How can you say that?"

His heart cracked at her question.

"How can you think otherwise?" he countered.

"You left me."

There it was. He had left her. How could he ever make her understand that he'd left for her own good, for their baby's good? She hadn't grown up in his house, hadn't heard the fights, felt the blame, the guilt. No, Savannah's parents had loved each other and her until the day her father had died. Her mother had continued to shower her with love every day since.

"Your mother is here."

Her gaze shifted, looking for her.

"Not here in Recovery, but in the waiting area."

Her cracked lips formed a semblance of an "O".

"Your cousin drove your mother and aunt up."

She stared at him but didn't say anything, just took a few more deep breaths.

"They're anxious to see you. Dr. Trenton says that once you are settled into a room he will let them visit."

"Did I lose our baby?"

Did she not know? Had no one told her? Or had she just forgotten or thought they'd lied to keep her spirits up? Was she unaware of the baby heart monitor beeping just as it should?

Then again, she'd sustained trauma and could have been told a dozen times and still not recall at this stage in her recovery.

"The fetal monitor is real, the results are real. Our baby is hanging in there."

She seemed to consider his comment a few minutes, then her worried gaze met his. "Am I going to miscarry?"

He didn't want to have this conversation with her. Not now. Not ever.

"I don't know, Savannah. I hope not."

"Why? Why would you care one way or the other? You don't want our baby."

Her words stung. Stung deep.

"I never said that."

"But you don't."

"I don't want you to miscarry, Savannah." Odd, as the best thing for her would be for her to be free of him completely. Yet he knew how much she wanted this baby. He'd seen it on her face in Chattanooga. He saw it now.

"They will do everything they can to keep you from miscarrying. If you do end up delivering, you couldn't be at a better neonatal unit than at Vander-bilt to increase our baby's chances of survival."

"Too early," she mouthed.

It was, but he wasn't going to confirm her fears.

"Babies are surviving at earlier and earlier gestation." Yes, they both knew the statistics weren't great and that the risks of complications were high.

Savannah didn't answer, just grunted, and closed her eyes.

Her alarm sounded again.

"Take a deep breath, Savannah."

"No," she countered but did so anyway, her sats immediately responding in a positive manner.

"Is there anything I can get you?" he asked, wishing there was something he could do to ease her pain and suffering. Wishing he could have somehow taken her place and be the one lying in the hospital bed instead of her.

"I don't want anything from you." It was the clearest sentence she'd said since he'd entered the recovery room area.

His gaze met hers.

"I was… I was coming to tell you…to give back your house."

What she said registered.

She was here because of him.

If he hadn't given her the house she wouldn't have driven to Nashville, wouldn't have been on I-24 when her car got struck, wouldn't by lying in this hospital bed recovering from serious injuries.

This was his fault.

He might not have been the one driving the car that slammed into Savannah, but it had been his fault she'd been in the wrong place at the wrong time.

Just as his mother's wreck had been his fault.

"I'm sorry, Savannah." He was. So very sorry.

She didn't respond to his apology, just closed her eyes.

"I'm so sorry," he repeated, this time a little louder.

"Just go," she finally said, her eyelids not budging. "Just leave me alone."

Savannah's head hurt, but as far as she could tell her brain was working. It was working, right? Because she was telling Charlie to go away.

Okay, so what she wanted to do was beg him to hold her, to let her cry over her pain, over her aches, over how scared she'd been when she'd braked, the moment of relief when she'd gotten stopped prior to ramming the car in front of her, then the sheer terror when she'd felt the impact, and then again. She wanted his comfort over the fear she might lose their baby.

She didn't want to lose their baby.

Despite how heavy her hand and arm felt, she moved her hand to cup her abdomen. Several blankets were between her palm and her belly.

She wanted to move them but didn't seem capable so maybe her brain wasn't working so well after all because she was telling her hand to move, but her arm wasn't cooperating.

"Let me." Charlie pulled back the blankets and guided her hand to her slightly rounded belly.

She expected him to immediately pull away, but he didn't. Instead, his hand stayed there with hers.

On cue, their baby moved. Just the tiniest of flutters, but one that made Savannah's heart sing. She shifted her hand, placed Charlie's over where she'd felt the movement.

His hand rested there for several long moments, but moved away before anything happened.

Disappointment filled her that he'd moved before getting to feel the magic of their baby's movements. But more than that. Disappointment filled her that he was no longer touching her, that the comfort of his touch was gone.

His touch shouldn't comfort her. She didn't want him or trust him. His touch should enrage her.

Yeah, maybe she was wrong. She'd told him to go, yet she did want him there.

Her brain wasn't working at all.

Maybe she had a concussion.

Actually, she probably did have a concussion.

She'd had a hard hit, had whiplash.

What had they told her was wrong with her?

She didn't know. Maybe they hadn't told her. Maybe she was dreaming. After all, why would Charlie be standing over her with that look in his eyes?

That look that for so long she'd believed was one of love.

He didn't love her.

Yet, when she stared into his eyes, she'd swear there were unshed tears there, that there was such raw emotion that he must care about her.

But thinking about it, trying to figure it out when she hadn't been able to understand for months why he'd left, made her brain hurt worse.

Her brain already hurt enough. Too much.

"Take a deep breath, Savannah."

Annoyed, she took another deep breath. "Why are you still here?"

"I'll be here until I know you're okay."

"I'm okay."

"God, I hope so." He sounded so sincere that she couldn't stand it anymore.

"Go away, Charlie," she moaned. "You are nothing to me anymore so just go away."

She expected him to argue, to say something. He didn't say anything for so long that Savannah opened her eyes.

Her breath caught.

He was gone.

Had she just dreamed that he was there?

At this point, reality and non-reality all seemed to swirl together.

CHAPTER NINE

"I FEEL FINE," Savannah protested for the hundredth time and was mostly telling the truth. Yes, she hurt all over still, and especially her left lower leg, but every day she felt a little stronger than the day before. "I want to go home."

Although, not really. Not until she was one hundred percent sure she wasn't going to go into early labor. If that happened, she wanted to be in the hospital, where her baby could get immediate medical attention. Five days had gone by since her wreck and although she'd had several contractions, they'd stopped on their own each time. The obstetrician had started injections as a precautionary measure to more rapidly mature the baby's lungs and every day that she didn't go into labor was critical time for her baby to continue to develop.

"Leaving the hospital is not going to happen for at least another twenty-four hours," Dr. Kimble told her.

Twenty-four hours. That both excited and scared

her. She was ready to be home, back in Chattanooga, away from Nashville and wondering if she'd see Charlie that day. She hadn't since the recovery room. Which was her own doing. She couldn't remember much of their conversation, but she'd told him to leave. She hadn't wanted him there.

"Thank you. I'll let my family know so someone can be here to bring me back to Chattanooga tomorrow."

The doctor shook her head. "I don't want you that far away from the hospital for at least a week, preferably longer."

"A week?"

She nodded. "I want to check you closely until I'm sure you and the baby are stable."

"But I live in Chattanooga," she reminded her. "I can't make that drive back and forth."

She didn't even own a working car at the moment.

"You're right. You can't make that drive back and forth. You need to stay in Nashville."

She stared at the doctor. She didn't want to stay in Nashville. She wanted to go home. Driving back and forth sounded better and better.

"You don't have to drive back and forth. You can stay at my place."

Savannah hadn't seen Charlie since the recovery room. For a while, she had truly questioned if he'd been there or if she'd imagined him. But her mother had commented on how he'd kept vigil in the waiting area, how he'd called her, how he'd arranged for a room at the Loew's Plaza Hotel and paid for it.

Her mother had gone home last night, fatigue overcoming her and Savannah insisting she go home. Under protest she had, but had called to check on her several times today.

Chrissie and a couple of the nurses from the cardiology floor had driven up to visit earlier in the week, and several other coworkers had called to check on her.

But until this moment she'd not seen or heard from Charlie.

The high-risk obstetrician didn't seem taken aback by Charlie's presence, which told Savannah that he'd been communicating with the specialist. Perhaps that should upset her, but at this point she didn't care.

"That's preferable to her driving back and forth two hours each way," the obstetrician agreed. "She'll need to be confined to bed rest, of course."

"Of course," Charlie agreed.

"There are excellent specialists in Chattanooga," Savannah pointed out, annoyed that the two were making decisions about her as if she weren't right there in the room and capable of making decisions for herself. She might have been in a major automobile accident and suffered a concussion, but she hadn't lost her mind. Not yet, anyway.

"Agreed, but I'd like to keep a check on you myself and I'd prefer you not to be in a car for the two plus hours each way. You need rest, not an exhausting ride."

"Two hours isn't an exhausting ride. Not really," she argued, despite knowing she'd do whatever was best for her baby.

"Regardless, I'd rather keep you here longer than for you to travel far from the hospital."

Did they really expect her to agree to stay at Charlie's? If circumstances were different she might suspect a set-up, but Charlie had left her, not the other way around.

Why would he volunteer to let her stay? Guilt?

"I will stay in Nashville," she agreed without actually agreeing to stay at Charlie's. Yes, she'd do whatever she had to do to protect her baby, but staying at Charlie's wasn't required to do that.

Only perhaps it was.

The only way Dr. Kimble would agree to release her to leave the hospital the next day was with the understanding that she would be under Dr. Keele's care. Hello, he was a cardiologist, not an obstetrician. It wasn't as if he was trained to deliver babies or to take care of pregnant women. He wasn't. Still, they were Dr. Kimble's conditions.

Not happy with the arrangement, Savannah allowed the nurse to wheelchair her out to Charlie's car, allowed Charlie to stow the bag of her things Chrissie had brought to her when she'd visited, allowed the nurse to assist her into Charlie's car.

It hit her again at that moment that she no longer had a vehicle. Hers was demolished. At some point she'd have to deal with her auto insurance carrier, with buying a new car, with getting behind the steering wheel and not thinking of the crash.

Her head hurt at the thought.

She'd deal with that later.

She settled back into the seat and closed her eyes.

"It's just as well I live so close. Dr. Kimble wants you to keep your legs up as much as possible."

"I don't think sitting in a car is going to cause me any problems."

"There's no reason to take any chances."

She kept her eyes squeezed shut and didn't respond. What was the point? For the next few days, maybe the next week, she was stuck as Charlie's house guest.

Charlie settled Savannah onto the sofa. With her feet propped up on one end and several pillows on the other, she lay there looking pale and much too quiet.

He'd half expected her to argue at every point, but she hadn't. She hadn't responded with anything more than one-word responses and a few thank-yous.

Not so long ago he'd felt closer to Savannah than anyone in the world. Now, in many ways, a stranger lay on his sofa.

A stranger because the withdrawn, obviously in pain woman wasn't the woman he'd known in Chattanooga. Not even close.

He'd done that to her.

Not directly.

But he was responsible for her pregnancy, for her unhappiness, for her being on that interstate.

He'd only been trying to help.

Just as his father had only been trying to help

when he'd married Charlie's mother. That hadn't turned out so well.

Neither had Charlie's involvement in Savannah's life.

Perhaps he should have hired a nurse to take care of her twenty-four-seven. He sort of had.

What would she think of the fact that he had hired her friend Chrissie to care for her while he was at work?

She surely would appreciate that he hadn't hired a stranger to stay with her. Her mother had thought it a good idea and given her blessing. Plus, Chrissie had jumped at the opportunity to make what he'd offered to pay her to stay with Savannah. Fortunately, the nurse had just worked four twelve-hour shifts in a row and was off for the next four days. Charlie had hired her for three of those four days. She would be with Savannah while he was at work through Friday. He was off work and call this weekend. He'd care for Savannah himself on Saturday and Sunday, had rearranged his schedule so he could go with her to her appointments with Dr. Kimble and Dr. Trenton on Monday. They'd figure out what needed to happen from there.

Regardless, he'd make sure she was taken care of. Always.

Which might not be his right.

It wasn't even now.

But he felt responsible for her, for their baby.

He wanted to take care of her.

And their baby.

Which was why he'd paid for a hotel room for Chrissie and her son for them to go to in the evenings after he got home. He'd take care of Savannah and their baby while he was home from work. Chrissie had agreed to return to his apartment if he had any emergencies and had to leave after hours.

He studied Savannah on the sofa. He'd given her a blanket, and she'd covered herself. She looked frail and banged up, with her black eye, bruised face and body, healing but still swollen lip, and bandaged leg.

"Can I get you anything?"

Without looking at him, she shook her head.

"Something to eat or drink?"

Again, she shook her head.

"Are you not going to talk to me?"

She opened her eyes, looked up. "What do you want me to say?"

Good question. What did he want her to say?

That she forgave him for doing this to her.

Only which *this* did he mean?

Her pregnancy or her car wreck? For being the same jerk his father had been? For not being able to give her the things she deserved?

He sank into a chair. "I'm not sure. I just don't like this awkwardness."

"You expected otherwise?"

"With us? Yes," he admitted, raking his fingers through his hair. "I guess I do. You and I should never be awkward."

"Why not?"

Another good question.

"Because of what we shared." Which really didn't make sense, even to his own ears. They were no longer a couple.

"What we shared no longer matters, Charlie. Haven't you figured that out yet?"

He understood what she was saying. She'd fancied herself in love with him. She was no longer under any false illusions, but that didn't mean they had to be enemies.

"You will always matter to me, Savannah," he admitted.

"Because of the baby?"

He thought for a moment. "The baby doesn't have anything to do with the fact that what we had was special. You were special."

Her lashes lowered as she looked away. "Not special enough."

"What's that supposed to mean?"

"I'm through with this conversation." She tugged the blanket up around her and turned her head away from him. "None of this matters anymore, Charlie. Not to me."

Frustrated, mostly with himself, Charlie sat in the chair and watched her, could tell the moment her tense body relaxed with sleep and she rolled back toward him. Still, he watched the rise and fall of the blanket, the peace that settled onto her bruised, swollen face.

A face that was more precious to him than any other.

A face that had haunted him.

He'd gotten so attached to Savannah that he'd recognized letting her go was going to be difficult. So he'd taken the decision out of his hands by doing something he'd known would upset her and make her push him away.

He'd purposely flubbed up his relationship with Savannah, making her hate him, because, deep down, he'd worried whether or not he'd be able to do right by her and walk away.

* * *

Savannah woke with a pressing need to go to the bathroom. Opening her eyes, it took her a moment to remember where she was.

Charlie's apartment.

In Charlie's living room. On Charlie's sofa. With Charlie asleep in a chair a few feet away.

The soft rise and fall of his chest mesmerized her. She struggled to tear her gaze away from his relaxed body. Tears pricked her eyes. She'd never thought she'd see him sleeping again. Had never dreamed she'd be staying in his Nashville apartment, that he'd be taking care of her.

She still didn't fully understand why she was here, why he was shifting his life around to accommodate her.

Guilt?

Probably.

Was that why he'd deeded her the house?

Why he'd volunteered to keep her at his apartment?

Because he felt guilty that she'd loved him and he hadn't felt the same? That she was pregnant with a baby he didn't want?

Didn't he realize none of that mattered now?

She no longer loved him and didn't need him to help her with the baby. She had this. Or she had before her wreck, and soon enough she'd be back on her feet and have her life back under control.

Trying to make as little noise as possible, she scooted up on the pillow, then slowly sat up, wincing in pain as she did so. Her eyes stayed on the sleeping man.

He didn't really look as if the past month had been overly good to him. He looked tired. Plus, he'd lost weight from his already lean frame, making his face look a little gaunt.

Her bladder reminded her of why she'd awakened. She'd toured the apartment with him prior to his leasing it so she knew where the guest bathroom was. She hated to wake Charlie to help her to the toilet when she'd be just fine going by herself. She preferred going by herself.

She didn't need him for that either.

Gritting her teeth to keep from groaning at the pain, she slowly stood from the sofa, made sure she wasn't tangled in the blanket, then hobbled to the bathroom.

See, she had this, and hadn't needed him at all.

* * *

Charlie woke with a start, his eyes immediately going to the sofa.

The empty sofa.

Savannah was gone.

"Savannah?" he called, leaping out of his chair. "Savannah?"

"Here," she answered, calming his racing heart as she limped into the living room. "I had to go to the bathroom."

"You should have woken me."

"Why?" she asked, settling back onto the sofa without taking the hand he offered. "I've been going to the bathroom by myself for more than two decades."

"Why can't you accept my help?"

"I am accepting your help. I'm here, aren't I? But I refuse to be treated like an invalid. I can see myself to the bathroom without you hovering over me."

"Point taken, but for the record I want to hover over you."

"Why?" she asked, staring at him pointedly. When he didn't immediately answer, she shook her head. "Never mind. Forget I asked. I don't want to know."

Which was just as well because he didn't know the answer—just that he wanted to take care of her.

"Are you hungry?"

She didn't look interested in food. Or much of anything else other than closing him out. "Not really, but I know I need to eat for the baby."

"And for you," he reminded.

She shrugged. "The baby is more important."

Charlie didn't respond because she wouldn't like his answer. "What would you like?"

"Just whatever you have is fine."

"My housekeeper grocery shopped today. I put several items I knew you like on her list. I can make you pretty much anything."

"Make me a fairy princess," she said without looking at him and without any inflection in her voice.

"Let me clarify," he began. "I can make you anything to eat you want. If I don't have whatever it is you're hungry for, I can run down the street and pick it up at the grocery store on the corner."

"Just something light would be good. I really don't want to be a bother. Maybe some eggs and toast?"

She wasn't a bother. Far from it. He was glad she was there, that he was able to do something to help, something to stop himself feeling so helpless, something to help amend all the wrong he'd done.

"With strawberry jam?" he offered, knowing she loved the stuff.

Her face perked up. "You have strawberry jam?"

Bingo.

"I do as of this morning."

"Then, yes, I'd like jam with my toast."

Charlie had waited on her hand and foot for the past couple of evenings. Her friend Chrissie had sat with her during the daytime, which was great and gave Savannah someone to spill her heart to.

"Being here is driving me crazy," she moaned. "How am I supposed to forget the man when I'm staying at his house?"

"Doesn't matter. You weren't forgetting Charlie when you were in Chattanooga and he was here."

Savannah frowned at where her friend sat on the floor playing with her two-year-old son. She started to argue that she was, but Chrissie didn't look as if she'd believe her. "Sure I was. But it helped when I wasn't having to look at him every night."

Chrissie's eyes widened. "He's sleeping in here?"

"Only because I'm in his bed and he hasn't set up the guest bedroom yet. I tried to get him to let me stay on the sofa, but he said he didn't want me lying on the sofa day and night." Because he was being thoughtful. *Ugh.* This would be easier if he wasn't being so nice. If he was being a jerk, like he was in Chattanooga, she could tell herself she was better off without him. She was better off without him. He'd told her point blank that she didn't matter as much as his career did. He'd left her when she'd thought things were perfect. "So," she continued, "I'm in his bed night after night. It's torture being here."

Chrissie snapped two blocks together and handed them to Joss. "Because it's where you want to be?"

Okay, so she wasn't as immune to the man as she'd like to be. This wasn't breaking news. But she didn't want to be here.

"I know his housekeeper changed the bedding before my arrival, but the room smells like him. This whole apartment smells like him. Everywhere I look, every breath I take, he's there. I'm surrounded by him," she whined. "And, even though I can't stand him, it is torture to have to be here when he's pretending to be all nice."

Helping with another two blocks, Chrissie laughed. "Keep telling yourself you can't stand him, if you must, but you still have it bad, girl."

"No, I don't. I took my heart back when he made the decision to move from Chattanooga without so much as a word to me first."

Chrissie shrugged, eyeing her son. "Since when does the heart just let us take it back when it's convenient? The heart knows what it wants even when our brain tells us otherwise."

Savannah eyed her friend, grateful for what she heard in her voice because it distracted her from her own woes.

"You never told me about Joss's dad," she gently reminded.

"Yeah, well, that's because he isn't what my heart wants so don't go getting ideas about me," Chrissie warned. "He was just a guy I met in Atlanta at a charity fundraiser we'd both volunteered at. I never saw him again. He hasn't been at the annual fundraiser since so I don't imagine I ever will."

Interesting that her friend had obviously thought he might be. "He worked in the medical profession?"

"I think he was a nurse or a paramedic. I don't know." Chrissie shrugged. "He was working triage so I guess he could have been anything." Her friend gave a wicked little smile. "We really didn't talk much."

Interesting. It was difficult to imagine her friend hooking up with a man she didn't know. Chrissie had barely dated prior to Joss being born and almost never now that she had her son. "A wild weekend, I take it?"

Chrissie's smile faded. "A weekend where I forgot who I was and just went with the flow. Look where that got me." She gestured toward her son, who looked up at her and grinned a grin destined to break a million hearts someday. Chrissie's face lit with love.

"Right where you wouldn't trade lives with anyone," Savannah reminded her. "He's precious."

Chrissie smiled and leaned forward to kiss the top of Joss's head. "That's true. I love this little guy more than anything."

Savannah was going to feel the same way about her baby. She already did. Her and Charlie's baby. Could she fully love her child and detest the father? She sighed. "I've got to make some type of peace with him, haven't I?"

"It's not like you're at war. He wants to be a part of your life."

"No, he doesn't," she denied. "He moved to get away from me."

Chrissie's brow rose at Savannah's claim. "He

moved to take a ridiculously awesome career opportunity."

Savannah frowned. "Whose side are you on?"

"I'm not picking sides."

Savannah waved her hand as if trying to get Chrissie's attention. "Hello. Best friend here. You're automatically supposed to be on my side."

"Let me point out to you that the man took care of your mother while she sat at the hospital with you, and that he kept vigil at the hospital while you recovered. And, oh, yeah, he even deeded you his house in Chattanooga. And we're not talking a shack. We're talking about a gorgeous home in a great neighborhood. Not that I'm taking sides..."

Yeah, there was all that. There was also that she'd thought they were wonderful and she'd been wrong, that he'd betrayed her trust, betrayed her heart, and that she would never trust him again. "Am I supposed to be impressed?"

"I'm impressed," Chrissie admitted.

"I'm impressed." Joss repeated his mother's words and both women smiled at the boy who was otherwise ignoring them and building a fort with his blocks.

"I'll also point out he brought you to his home so he could take care of you and, best of all, he's paying me a load of money to do something I offered to do for free."

"I wouldn't have let you do that," Savannah pointed out, considering all her friend said.

"Neither would he."

"So, he has a few redeeming qualities."

Chrissie arched a brow. "A few?"

"Need I remind you that, despite those redeeming qualities, he made the decision to move to Nashville without even mentioning the possibility to his girlfriend—me—who he'd been seriously dating for a year?"

"I haven't forgotten."

Savannah frowned. "You've decided that was okay?"

"No." Chrissie's brows rose. Joss climbed into her lap and ran his little finger along the bunched skin between her eyes. Chrissie took his hand and kissed his fingertip over and over, making him giggle and wrap his little arms around her. "What I've decided is that I'm sticking with my original thoughts. He's crazy about you, but works for the CIA and is on a secret assignment."

"You and your secret agent theory." She rolled her eyes. "He doesn't work for the CIA. He's a cardiologist. He had a great job. Yes, maybe this one is better, but he doesn't act as if he's happier here."

"Maybe he's not." She punctuated her sentence with a kiss to Joss, who still hugged her. "Maybe he realizes he made a huge mistake. Maybe, rather than shutting him out, you need to remind him of how good it was between you two."

Savannah put her hand over her belly, thinking that before long she'd be the one loving and being loved by her child. The thought made her heart sing.

"That's a lot of maybes, the biggest one being that maybe I want him back. I don't."

"You're right," Chrissie agreed. "It is a lot of maybes. It's obvious he has strong feelings for you."

Her heart squeezing a little, she asked, "How is that obvious?"

"Savannah, have you paid attention to how he looks at you? I've said it before but it bears repeating. I'd give my right arm for a man to look at me the way Charlie Keele looks at you."

"That's…" She stopped. Lust? She wasn't exactly what dreams were made of. Perhaps she never had been, but especially not now, with her black eye, bruised, swollen face, healing leg, and pregnant belly.

"That's what?" Chrissie asked, tickling Joss and causing him to twist and turn in her arms.

"I don't know. I started to say that it was just sexual attraction, but I'm about as far from sexy as a woman could be."

"Don't even think that man doesn't want you, because he does. It shows in how he watches your every move."

She wasn't sure if Chrissie's observation disappointed her or thrilled her. Maybe a little of both. She might be physically recovering from her wreck, but she wasn't dead. Her body reacted every time Charlie was near. "So you think this is still just about sex?"

"I didn't say that."

"Then what?" she asked in exasperation.

"I think you need to set aside your pride for the remainder of time you are here and remind Charlie what he lost."

"You think I should seduce him? Hello, even if I wanted to, which I don't," she quickly added, "look at me."

Chrissie ignored her protest. "Pride, or whatever it is keeping you two apart, needs to be set aside to give whatever feelings are there a chance to flourish."

"We had a year to flourish," Savannah reminded her. They had flourished. Then he'd killed them. "I don't need him, Chrissie. I'm better off without him."

"You have the rest of your life to regret not opening yourself up to the possibility that maybe Charlie was more torn about his decision than you give him credit for. Maybe his taking the job was a test to see if you'd go with him. Or maybe it was a test to see if he'd get over you. Or maybe—"

"Or maybe he did exactly what he wanted and my being pregnant threw a big ole wrench in his plans to move on with his life and he feels guilty that he knocked me up."

"Maybe." Chrissie kissed Joss's forehead, then was the recipient of a very wet smack to her lips, smushed together between his little hands.

"Again, that's a lot of maybes."

Chrissie nodded. "All I'm saying is that I think you need to set the chip on your shoulder aside and just remember this is the man you are in love with and this may be your last opportunity to show him the error of his ways."

"Apparently you aren't hearing a thing I'm saying. I'm not in love with him, and you mean I should fight for him, but why shouldn't he be the one fighting for me?"

"Maybe in his own way he is," Chrissie suggested.

"He left me." Did she sound as whiny as she felt?

Chrissie didn't look sympathetic. "You let him."

"I couldn't have stopped him."

Chrissie just gave her an expectant look that said she didn't believe her.

"I couldn't have," she repeated, knowing it was true. She hadn't mattered enough for Charlie to stay. Besides, even if she could have, Charlie had wanted to go, to pursue his dreams. "I wouldn't have."

"Because you love him," Chrissie said matter-of-factly. "When he comes home, remind yourself of that, remind him of that."

Savannah frowned. "I'm not telling him anything of the sort." She sure wasn't reminding herself of something that wasn't even true. She didn't still love him. She didn't. She couldn't. Wouldn't.

"Don't tell him," Chrissie smugly suggested. "Show him."

CHAPTER TEN

CHARLIE'S DAY HAD been busy. He liked busy days. Normally. Today, he'd just wanted to go to the apartment he called home.

Not that the place had felt much like home. It hadn't. Maybe because he'd bought the place in Chattanooga and grown so comfortable there. It had been a great house, a great yard, a great neighborhood. A place for settling down and staying forever.

Not that he'd ever meant to do that. He hadn't. He'd bought it as an investment. The place had been marked way below market value for a quick sale due to a bank foreclosure.

The house would be a home, would have love and happiness inside it. With Savannah and their son or daughter.

He closed his eyes and tried to imagine him in the house with them and couldn't. He wasn't destined for such happiness.

But Savannah was and he'd do what he could to make sure she and their child had all their physical needs met.

His child would grow up with a loving mother, with a peaceful home, with lots of love and happiness. It was the best gift he could give.

The gift he would give.

"Dr. Keele, there's a hot load coming in. You're needed in the heart lab." The nurse filled him in on the patient's details. "Dr. Sansbury and Dr. Louwitz are both already tied up. That leaves you on call this evening."

Glancing at his watch, he nodded. "Thanks. I'll head that way and get scrubbed up."

He didn't want to go to the cath. lab or anywhere that had anything to do with his career. He wanted to go to his apartment.

He wanted to go to where Savannah was.

Home.

No. Savannah wasn't home. He couldn't do that to her. He just couldn't. Not now or ever. Having her at his apartment made him forget things he needed to remember. Savannah deserved better than someone like him and it was time he reminded her of that.

* * *

"He's not going to come home after all," Savannah mused to her friend.

"Sure he is. You said he texted that he got a call about a procedure."

He had texted that he'd gotten called into doing an emergency cath. But that had been hours and hours ago.

"It's after eight."

"He'll be home."

On cue, the apartment door rattled with Charlie's key.

Both women glanced up. Savannah lay on the sofa and Chrissie sat with a sleeping Joss against her chest. The little boy had given up about twenty minutes before and dozed off.

"Sorry I'm late," Charlie said to no one in particular as he came into the apartment.

"It's not a problem," Chrissie assured him.

Savannah didn't say anything. What could she say? She was a guest in his home and he'd gotten tied up at work. Despite her whining to Chrissie, she had no rights here.

"He's asleep?" Charlie asked, gesturing to the little boy.

"We wore him out today playing."

"That's good."

When Chrissie went to stand, still holding her son, Charlie came over to her. "Can I help you?"

Chrissie shook her head. "Nope. I'm leaving his bag and things here for in the morning. I've got extras at the hotel."

"I hate that you are staying at a hotel. Are you sure you don't want to just stay?" Savannah offered, thinking she probably shouldn't be inviting someone to stay at an apartment that wasn't hers. Her anxiety over being alone with Charlie was enough that she did so without hesitation, though.

Charlie didn't say anything, just waited for Chrissie to respond.

"No, I'm good and like my time with this little guy. I will see you in the morning." Chrissie made a puckered lip face toward Savannah, blowing a kiss without using her hands as they were full of her son. "I will let you hand me my purse."

Charlie glanced toward where she gestured, then grabbed the pocketbook. "You're sure there's nothing else I can do?"

"Maybe get the doors for me to make it easier, but, regardless, I can do this. We single moms get good at these kinds of things."

As Charlie first opened the apartment door and

then her car door so she could put the child in his car seat, it struck him that Savannah would be a single mom. She'd have to maneuver their child from one place to another without help.

Because he wouldn't be there.

He winced at the thought and reminded himself of all the reasons why he'd moved to Nashville to begin with.

Chrissie snapped Joss's seat, checked to make sure the connection was secure, then she straightened, turned to Charlie.

"Be nice to her."

Charlie frowned. "Do you think I need to be told to be nice?"

"Do you?" she asked, giving him a look that said she thought he did. "She's been through a lot and I don't just mean the wreck."

"Me?"

Still standing by Joss's open car door, Chrissie shrugged. "You hurt her pretty bad."

"That was never my intention."

She nodded. "I believe that, which is why I still like you. Just make sure you don't hurt her more."

"You think she shouldn't be here? That I shouldn't be taking care of her right now?"

"That depends."

"On?"

"On what your intentions are."

"I have no intentions." He didn't, except to make sure she didn't live the life his mother had lived.

Chrissie studied him in the dim light of the parking lot. "If you truly mean that, then you shouldn't be taking care of her. You should have stayed away. Maybe you should ask yourself why you didn't."

Charlie wanted to ask what she meant, but Chrissie just walked around the car and opened the driver's side door.

"I'll see you in the morning. Oh, and by the way, I don't believe you on the 'no intentions' comment."

With that she closed the door and drove away.

"Did she get off okay?" Savannah asked when Charlie came back into his apartment.

"She did." He sat down in the chair Chrissie had vacated minutes before and stared at the woman propped up on his sofa.

"Long day?" she asked, studying him as closely as he was studying her.

"It was." Too long. "I'm sorry I was late."

"You don't have to apologize," she advised. "You owe me nothing."

"Perhaps I do."

"What do you mean?"

He raked his fingers through his hair. "Ignore me. I'm tired and talking out of my head."

"Have you eaten? Chrissie made a casserole. It's in the kitchen if you're hungry."

He hadn't eaten. His stomach seemed to suddenly remember that and growled. "Casserole sounds fabulous. I'm starved."

"Did you eat lunch?"

He thought back and couldn't recall eating.

When he didn't answer, Savannah shook her head. "No wonder you've lost weight."

"A few pounds."

"You didn't need to lose weight. You were perfect as you were." Realizing what she'd said, she backtracked. "I mean...you know what I mean."

He gave a tired smile. "I do, and thank you. How's the pain tonight?"

She shrugged. "Bearable."

"I admire your resolve to not take anything for the baby's sake."

"It's not worth the risk."

"I hate to see you suffer."

"I'm okay." She was. Or at least she would be. Eventually. Her leg, that was. When she looked at Charlie she wasn't so sure about other areas. Perhaps when you'd loved as deeply as she'd loved Charlie you never really healed.

After he'd eaten, he asked, "You want to watch a movie?"

Surprised at his suggestion, Savannah glanced up. "A movie?"

"I could rent something online for us to watch."

"If that's what you want to do."

She'd obviously not hidden her reluctance because he asked, "You don't?"

She laughed a little lamely. "I'm just sitting here with this leg propped up following doctor's orders. Whatever you want to do is fine."

"We could do something else if you'd like," he offered; being that thoughtful guy again was making it so difficult to remember that he'd walked away from her so coldly. Walls began slamming up all around her and she shook them off. No, she wasn't going to shut him out. Tonight she'd just pretend that all the negative hadn't happened. She'd not question her motives too closely and she'd just do her best to relax and rejoice that she was alive, that her baby was alive, that she was with a man who once upon a time had made her feel like the luckiest woman in the world and that, for better or worse, she was going to have a baby with him.

She named a card game they'd played numerous times in the past, sometimes just the two of them, sometimes with friends.

He looked surprised. "You want to play cards?"

She nodded. She would rather play cards than watch a movie. Playing a game, she wouldn't have to try to think of anything to say and yet they would talk. After all, if she was going to be here for a few more days, they needed some sort of truce.

"Yes, I'd like to play cards." She smiled what was her first real smile at him for months. "I like beating you."

Surprise flitted across his face and his brow arched. "You don't beat me at cards."

Good eyebrow arched, she tsked. "I might have been the one with a concussion, but it's your memory failing. I always win when we play cards."

He studied her a moment, his eyes intense in their darkness, his expression just as deep. Then his features softened and the corner of his mouth inched upward. "Right. You do." His smile came on full force. "When you're my partner."

Savannah's breath caught in her chest and she was grateful the pulse oximeter monitor was no longer monitoring her because the alarm bell would be sounding. *Breathe, Savannah, breathe.*

"Ooh, that was sneaky," she chided, her gaze not leaving his. "And not true."

"We'll see." His smile fell. "Or we would, except I don't have any cards here."

"Good thing for you I do." She reached into the bag that Chrissie had brought her. Inside were romance novels, puzzle books, an adult coloring book and pencils, cards, a learn-to-knit kit, and several other occupy-her-time-while-recuperating items her friend had given her. She pulled out the card box and waved it in front of her. "Because I'm awesome that way."

His lips curved in a smile and he looked more relaxed while awake than she'd seen him in months. "Yeah, you are awesome that way, but you are still going to lose."

Nope. He was wrong. Whether she toppled him in cards or not, she had won. Because he was kneeling down to sit on the floor on the opposite side of the coffee table and they were smiling at each other. That definitely made her feel like the winner.

She just wasn't sure why she felt that way.

Chrissie's time was up and she wouldn't be coming back to stay with Savannah. Which was just as well. Savannah felt able to take care of herself, despite the way Charlie treated her as if she were a fragile invalid.

Yes, she still hobbled around and looked like someone had beat her with a stick, but she felt stronger each day.

Plus, it was Friday and her baby had gotten in another week without being born. Every day was so critical. Plus, with each passing day the odds of going into premature labor decreased.

"I brought Chinese," Charlie announced, entering the apartment with a plastic bag full of food. "I hope that's okay."

"I told you in my text that Chinese was fine," she reminded him. She'd be glad when he quit being so accommodating. Accommodating Charlie was too much like Pre-Leaving for Nashville Charlie, and it was too easy to forget they were no longer a couple.

"Yeah, but I thought you might have changed your mind."

"About Chinese?" She frowned. "Never."

"I'm glad your appetite is back. I wasn't the only one who'd lost weight."

"I hadn't lost weight. It was just distributed a little differently."

"Even naked I didn't immediately realize," he mused.

She gave him a *duh* look. "That's because you were naked and distracted."

"True, but I can't believe I didn't straight away notice."

"I was only three months pregnant, barely showing, and even I forgot I was pregnant," she admitted, a bit stunned that she was doing so. "I'd never have kissed you or let you take me to the bedroom if I'd been thinking clearly."

His expression tightened and she realized what she'd said and went to clarify.

"It wasn't that I didn't want you, Charlie. I did." She still did, but she'd keep that to herself. "I just wouldn't have chosen for you to find out I was pregnant that way."

His expression remained terse. "Sometimes I wonder if you wanted me to find out at all."

She understood why he felt that way. She'd known two months without telling him. Two months when she'd agonized back and forth and came to the same conclusion. How could she tell him prior to his move without him thinking that she was trying to force him to stay? So, right or wrong, she'd kept her news to herself. "I would have told you.

Doing otherwise was never a real option. I just thought it best if I waited until you were settled in your new life."

He leaned back against the sofa, closed his eyes, and seemed to take in what she was saying. "I'm sorry, Savannah."

Her throat tightened. "For?"

He half shrugged. "Putting you in this situation."

"Again—" she searched for the right words "—it's not how I would have chosen and certainly wasn't intentional, but I always wanted children. Our baby is a blessing. At least, that's how I see it."

The skin pulled tight over his cheekbones and if she didn't know better she'd swear his eyes looked glassy.

"Not everyone thinks that way."

His words stung deep. No, she imagined he didn't think that way. This pregnancy was a major inconvenience to him.

She was a major inconvenience to him.

Which she hated. She just wanted to go home. If it weren't for the baby, she would beg Chrissie to come get her.

Something that should be so beautiful, so wonderful, wasn't. Not to him. She refused to let him keep stealing her joy at becoming a mother. He didn't want to be a part of her and the baby's life. Fine. "I don't expect anything from you."

She didn't want anything from him. Sure, she wanted her baby to have a father's love, but if he couldn't give that, then so be it. She'd love their baby enough for the both of them.

Charlie sucked in a deep breath. "It's the expectations I have of myself that are the problem."

Trying to calm the anger surging through her, she took a deep breath. "What are your expectations of your role with our child?"

He closed his eyes and shook his head back and forth. "Financially, I'll take care of you and the baby."

She let what he'd said sink in. "I don't want your money."

"It would be unfair on you not to give our child the advantages I can provide."

"You gave me your house, Charlie. That wasn't necessary."

"To me, it was. I don't want you to worry about where you raise our child."

Where she raised their child.

"I can give our baby everything he or she needs," she assured him, daring him to claim otherwise. Chrissie did it, and did it well. She could, too.

Charlie shook his head. "I will help you financially, but otherwise it would be best if I stay out of the picture as much as possible."

A vice gripped her heart and squeezed it dry. Money. That was what he was offering their child. Not fatherly love. Not to be there to see a first smile, hear a first word, witness a first step. Money.

Disgust filled her.

"Best for who? Our baby? How is it best for a child not to know his or her father?"

His face was ashen, his eyes hollow pits of pain that poked holes in her anger. "Not all fathers are worth knowing."

What he said sank in and she realized how little she truly knew of his childhood. He didn't talk about his parents. Never. She knew they'd both passed on but, other than that, nothing. "Was your father not a good father?"

His lips twisted wryly and he shook his head. "Not on his best day."

"I'm sorry."

His shoulders lifted, fell in a half-hearted shrug. "It's no big deal."

But obviously it was and she wanted to ask more, to know more, to understand him, but he seemed done with their too emotional conversation. He stood from the chair and picked up the empty food containers.

"You need anything?"

She shook her head and watched him disappear into the kitchen, knowing he wasn't capable of giving her what she needed.

Savannah was getting around better and better. Charlie didn't doubt that her specialists would soon release her to go back to Chattanooga. Perhaps they even would today at her appointments. Currently, they sat in Dr. Trenton's office, waiting for him to recheck her leg.

Charlie had wheeled her into the hospital in a wheelchair, but she was walking around his apartment more and more and depending on his help less and less. Mostly, she was still resting, following her obstetrician's recommendations, but otherwise Charlie felt she'd be pushing herself full force.

"Your leg is doing great," Dr. Trenton praised after he'd done pulse checks. "I'm very pleased with your progress. The repaired artery and the surrounding muscle tissue will continue to heal from the puncture wound. I'm releasing you from my care unless you have further issues."

"That's good news," Charlie immediately said,

earning him a glare from Savannah. One that said she'd misunderstood what he'd meant. She thought he was ready for her to leave.

He wasn't.

Despite her injuries and his guilt over the role he'd played, the happiest he'd been in Nashville had been since she'd arrived. He had no right to feel happy about her being there, though. It was his fault she had gone through all of this.

"I can go back to Chattanooga?" Savannah asked.

"As far as I'm concerned, yes. However, I wasn't the one holding you up," he reminded her. "Dr. Kimble will have the final say on when she thinks it's safe for you to venture that far from our neonatal unit."

Savannah nodded. "As ready as I am to go home, I want to do what's best for the baby even more."

Dr. Kimble wasn't as accommodating on Savannah's leaving.

"You were in a major automobile accident, suffered a great deal of trauma, and although, with each day that passes, your risk of premature labor and complications goes down, I do think it's too early for you to travel two hours away."

Savannah sighed, but didn't argue with the obstetrician. Her eyes ate up the monitor during her ultrasound, taking in every detail with an excited gleam in her eyes.

Charlie found it difficult to pull his gaze away from Savannah's face to actually look at the monitor, too.

Her face shone with joy. She was so in love with their child. She really did see their baby as a blessing. Her expression said so.

Had his own mother ever looked at his ultrasound with a similar expression? Somehow, Charlie didn't think so. He didn't doubt that she'd loved him in her own way. She had always seen to it that he had his basic needs met. But he wasn't so sure that she'd ever really wanted him.

Because of him she'd been trapped in a life married to a man who made her miserable, abused her verbally and, at the end, physically. Whatever dreams for her future she'd had were snatched away because of Charlie's very existence. Although his father had always been verbal about what he'd sacrificed for marriage and fatherhood, he couldn't recall his mother having mentioned what her plans had been prior to her pregnancy, just that he'd ruined her life by being born.

Now, Savannah's life was drastically changed

due to a pregnancy. Because of him, yet another person would have to give up their dreams.

"Everything looks and sounds good," Dr. Kimble praised Savannah as the baby's heartbeat echoed throughout the room.

That. Was. His. Baby's. Heart.

He tried to meet Savannah's gaze, but she refused.

"Try to stay off your feet as much as possible for at least another week and see me again on Monday, sooner if there are any problems. I plan to repeat an ultrasound at that time."

"I'm game for as many ultrasounds as you want to do," Savannah told Dr. Kimble as she pulled one of Charlie's sweatshirts down over her belly. Sitting up, she tugged the waistband of her yoga pants up, decided it was too tight, then slid it back down to rest beneath her belly.

"I love getting to see my baby."

Dr. Kimble smiled, handing Savannah a piece of paper. "Most women do."

"Thank you," she told the woman, took her appointment slip, and headed to the checkout desk.

When they got back into his car, Charlie pulled out of the hospital parking garage, but he ached inside.

His apartment was close. He usually walked to the hospital but, with Savannah supposed to stay off her feet as much as possible, walking wasn't an option and he'd taken his car. Traffic was heavy and they sat at a red light one traffic stop up from the turn to his place.

"Please don't make me go back to your apartment," she surprised him by saying.

He glanced toward her. She stared out the window at the hustle and bustle on the street despite the cool temperature.

"You heard Dr. Kimble—"

"I don't mean at all," she clarified, turning toward him. Her eyes were red, puffy, and not just from the remains of her wreck. "I mean right now. I know I still look frightful." She touched her face over her bruised, swollen cheekbone and eye. "But I am so tired of being cooped up there. Take me somewhere. Anywhere. Just not back inside that apartment."

"You don't look frightful." He glanced at his watch, gauging how much time he had before his afternoon appointments started. He'd rescheduled his morning, but not his afternoon. He had just under three hours before his first appointment. He'd allowed plenty of time because he hadn't been sure how long her appointments would take or if she'd need any further testing.

From the passenger seat, Savannah sighed. "Now I'm the one who is saying I'm sorry. I shouldn't have said that. I know you need to get back to the hospital. Thank you for taking off this morning to bring me to my appointments."

"I wanted to be there." He had. Soon she'd be strong enough to go back to Chattanooga and then he wouldn't be there for appointments. He'd miss out on so much.

"I want to be there when you have our baby." His words surprised him almost as much as they surprised her.

They did surprise him.

Her eyes big, she stared. "If that's what you want."

"I do." Surprisingly, he meant his words. He couldn't imagine not being there when their baby made his or her appearance into the world.

Which made no sense. Not being there made even less.

"Promise you'll call when you go into labor."

Still staring at him as if he'd grown a third eye, or worse, she nodded. "Anything else?"

He thought a moment. "Are we having a boy or a girl?"

She shrugged. "I don't know."

His eyebrows rose. "But the paper the sonographer gave you…"

"I never looked."

He arched his brow. "You didn't?"

She shook her head.

"Why not?"

She'd not hesitated in saying she wanted to know the gender of their baby. Why wouldn't she have looked?

"I decided I'd wait."

But he knew.

"You wouldn't be able to keep it a secret from me," he guessed. "So you opted not to find out, too."

Her face said he was right even as she continued to try to bluff him. "I thought we had already established that I'm better at keeping secrets than you're giving me credit for."

She was referring to her pregnancy, and she was right. He hadn't even suspected.

"Once I knew about the baby, keeping the gender from me would have been more difficult."

"Why?" she pushed. "Until my wreck, we didn't talk."

He winced. She was right. They hadn't.

"If I could go back in time…" His voice trailed off, mostly because he wasn't sure what he was going to say. Had he been about to say that he'd have talked to her? Insisted she talk to him? Or had he been implying something much more profound? Something he had no right to imply because he wouldn't change having left Chattanooga.

She seemed to sense that he himself didn't know because she didn't push him to elaborate despite the curiosity shining on her face.

"Where are we going?" she asked instead as they crossed over I-440.

"The mall."

"The mall?"

"You need new clothes."

She glanced down at her yoga pants and his sweatshirt. "Sorry, my clothing selection here in Nashville is limited."

"Which is why we're headed to the mall."

"I won't be here long enough to justify clothes shopping."

"You'll be here long enough for dinner tonight."

"Dinner?"

"I figure you're tired of takeout and my limited cooking skills. Although you look great in anything, I imagine you're ready for clothes that fit your growing body properly."

"Are you saying I'm getting too fat for my clothes?" she asked, a playful gleam in her eyes that told him she wanted to keep the peace between them as much as he did.

"You're not fat, Savannah. Far from it. But I did see you slide your waistband back down due to discomfort."

"The struggle is real." She patted her protruding belly. "But I have clothes that fit at home. Chrissie is going to bring me some on her next day off."

"No need. I'll get you whatever you need today." When she started to argue, he glanced her way, met her gaze for a brief second before refocusing on the road. "Let me do this, Savannah. I want to do this."

"I don't need you giving me things, Charlie."

He knew that, had never doubted it. "Let me anyway."

She hesitated, not wanting to say yes, but at least considering what he was saying. Finally, she sighed. "Okay. But I'm paying for anything I get. And, for the record, I'm not keeping the house."

He'd let her think that, but he planned to buy her

clothes. As far as the house, they'd save that discussion for another day. He whipped his car into the Green Hills mall parking area. He wasn't much of a mall person, but surely this place had maternity clothes.

CHAPTER ELEVEN

SAVANNAH STARED AT her reflection in the mirror. Odd that Charlie had bought her first real maternity clothes for her. A pair of black pants and a pair of jeans, both with stretchy front panels, a couple of nice tops, and the long-sleeved black dress she currently wore with the black boots and maternity support hose he'd also bought her.

She'd argued, but he'd insisted. The cashier had refused to take Savannah's credit card when Charlie had shoved cash at her. She'd considered refusing the purchases, but that would be childish.

She'd styled her hair, put on make-up from what Chrissie had brought her to cover her bruised face, and looked almost like a normal person. Almost.

With time her bruises would fade, already they were much improved from her wreck. Her swelling was going down. Her lacerations healing well and barely visible beneath her make-up.

Soon she would be able to go back to her old life.

The baby moved, shifting within her belly. She

wouldn't ever really be able to go back to her old life. Not really.

She didn't even want to.

Oh, she needed to get back to work as soon as possible. She'd planned to take time off after the baby's birth and having to use her paid time off days due to the wreck just wasn't good. Plus, whether she was working or not, she still had expenses such as water, electricity, rent.

She needed to get back to work.

Back in Chattanooga, reality still existed. Bills still existed. She needed to get back to reality.

She brushed the hair from her face, revealing where her sutures had been. The wound was healing well and barely noticeable, but she dropped the hair back, covering it. She wanted to look good, or at least the best she could.

Ridiculous, considering how different she looked from just a few months ago. She'd been at her best and he'd left. Nothing she could do was going to change that.

She no longer even wanted to change that.

The apartment door rattled with his key and she took one last look in the mirror at her reflection.

She didn't need him or anyone.

* * *

Charlie took one look at Savannah and let out a low wolf whistle. "You look great."

Her cheeks glowed a rosy red. "I did the best I could under the circumstances."

"Like I said, you look great." He walked to her, turned her slowly to inspect her new outfit. "A little loose, but another few weeks and you'll fill this out perfectly."

"At the rate I'm gaining weight, it may be too small in a few weeks." She laughed a little self-consciously.

"Savannah?" he said, hearing the doubt in her voice. "You know you're beautiful?"

She still wouldn't meet his eyes.

He tilted her chin upward, forcing her gaze to his. "You. Are. Beautiful."

She stared straight into his eyes, her own a little shiny. "Thank you."

Her lower lip quivered and something shifted inside his chest. Maybe his head too, because he bent to press his lips to hers. Gently because he didn't want to hurt her. Her busted lip appeared healed, but he didn't know how sore she still was.

She stood on tiptoe, met his kiss in a sweet caress that had him wanting to take her into his arms and do a lot more than just kiss her lips.

But he kept the kiss soft, kept his hands to himself, and pulled back, smiled down into her confused face, all the while reminding himself he had no right to kiss her.

He shouldn't be kissing her.

"You always had the most amazing mouth," he said instead of the apology he should be issuing. He had no rights. He'd done enough damage to Savannah, and yet…

"My mouth always felt pretty amazing when you were kissing it," she countered, her gaze searching his. She had questions, lots of questions.

Too bad he didn't have answers. He didn't. Not for her or himself.

For tonight, he'd just enjoy being in her company. He owed it to her and to himself to not let history repeat itself, but one night of not focusing on all the things he should be doing wasn't going to change a thing.

He took her hand and gave a reassuring squeeze. "Come on. Let me take you out to dinner and show you off to the world."

* * *

Savannah bit her lower lip as she stared at the man sitting across the table from her.

The candlelit table.

What was he doing?

Buying her clothes, taking her to a fabulous restaurant, and having them put at a private, almost romantic, booth.

This wasn't a romantic meal. He wasn't wooing her.

They were two people who'd had their chance at being a couple and they'd failed. He didn't want her and she didn't want him.

Offering her a piece of bread he'd just sliced from the fresh loaf the waiter had put on the table, he smiled. Really smiled. One that reached his eyes. One that dug dimples into his cheeks. One that set off explosions in her head.

She shouldn't be here. They shouldn't be here. They weren't a couple. They shouldn't be acting like one.

"Is that what we're doing?" she asked out loud.

His forehead scrunched as he tried to figure out what she meant.

"Acting like a couple?" she clarified.

Setting the bread back on the wooden cutting board, he considered her question.

"Acting implies a pretense. I'm not pretending, Savannah. We're not a couple. Just two people who used to enjoy each other's company. I still enjoy your company."

"This feels pretend."

"Why?"

"Because it feels reminiscent of the past."

"This is the here and now."

"I don't want you to get the wrong idea."

He laughed a little ironically. "I'm not going to get the wrong idea, Savannah. I know you hate me."

Was that what he thought? That she hated him?

"I don't hate you."

"Not yet."

"I can't imagine ever hating you, Charlie."

"It'll come."

"What makes you think that?"

"It's just what happens."

His answers made no sense to her. She stared at him from across the table. "Is that how you feel about me? That you hate me or that you're going to at some point in the future?"

He looked as if her question shocked him. "Why would you think that?"

"For the same reasons you think I'm going to hate you."

He shook his head. "You're a much better person than I am. I can't imagine anyone has hated you during your entire life."

The way he said it made her think someone had hated him. Someone who had hurt him dearly.

"Have you ever been in love, Charlie?"

"No." He stared at her as if she'd lost her mind. "Nor will I ever be. Some people aren't meant for such things."

"You're one of those people?"

He nodded.

"Why is that?" she pushed. "Are you heartless? Or just have so many walls that no woman can ever get through to you?"

"Neither. I'm just not capable."

For so long she'd believed otherwise. She'd believed he'd been in love with her. She'd have bet her life on it.

"What about you?"

She blinked at his question. "What about me about what?"

"Have you ever been in love?"

Besides him, he meant?

"No. I don't need a man, Charlie. I forgot that for a while with you, but the reality is I do just fine on my own. Always have. Always will."

"You're right. You're the strongest woman I know."

She wasn't that strong. Not really. But she'd fake it until she made it. Or something like that.

Their conversation remained light through the rest of their meal, mostly with Charlie telling her stories about his class at the university and the research he'd gotten involved with. All of which fascinated Savannah.

"How did you end up in cardiology?" she asked after the waiter had taken their dessert order.

"For as long as I can remember, I knew I was going to be a doctor. My grandfather had congestive heart failure and was in and out of the hospital with exacerbations. I remember sitting at his bedside with my mother. His cardiologist came in and I listened to him and knew at that moment that I wanted to specialize in cardiology. From that point on, I've never considered doing anything else."

"How old were you?"

"Eleven."

"You've known what you wanted to do since you were eleven years old?" she asked incredulously.

He nodded. "I've no regrets. I enjoy what I do."

A memory of the night he'd told her he was leaving for Nashville flashed through her mind. "That's right. Your career means everything to you."

Did it? Charlie wondered. If life were different, if he were different, he wasn't so sure he'd feel that way.

But life wasn't different. He wasn't different. He was a person his own parents hadn't loved. A person who had caused his own mother to take her life.

Yeah, it was much better for him to focus on his career.

He could control his career.

Emotions and relationships were things that were unpredictable. You couldn't make someone love you. He'd tried his entire childhood. And even if a person thought they loved you…he'd witnessed time and again over the years as "love" had faded into fights and eventually a breakup. He didn't fool himself that he was any better than his friends and colleagues. Eventually, he and Savannah would have reached crisis point and everything would have fallen apart. She'd have realized she didn't really care about him, that he was unlovable.

He'd just sped that process up by taking the job in Nashville. Only he'd been too late. He'd already gotten her pregnant.

"Do you have names picked out?"

Her gaze lifted to his and a myriad of emotions swam across the deep blue of her eyes. "Not really. Any family names you've always considered passing along to one of your kids?"

"I never planned to have children." He raked his hand through his hair. "I guess the responsible thing would have been for me to have had a vasectomy, but I thought we were always careful."

"I'm sorry I messed up your plans."

Her words cut deep, echoing how he'd felt most of his childhood, most of his life. Never did he want Savannah to feel that way, for their child to feel that way.

"It's my fault, not yours. But no, there's nothing I'd want to pass from my family to our child. My grandfather is the only pleasant memory I have of anyone related to me."

"The one who died when you were eleven?"

He nodded. "He was the only person who ever seemed to want me around."

"That's sad."

He shook his head. "Nope. That's life."

"Not my life."

"I'm glad you had a better upbringing, Savannah."

"It wasn't always easy. My parents were crazy about each other. When my dad died, my mother was devastated and suddenly struck with the reality that she didn't know how to do anything or how to take care of herself and me."

She paused, took a sip of her water. "While my mom devoted herself to me all day long every day, my dad worked, took care of the finances, the house, everything."

"That must have been hard on her, and you, after he died."

"Looking back, I think she would have had a mental breakdown if it weren't for having to take care of me. She pulled herself together and did what she had to do. She got a job at the school where I went so her schedule would be the same as mine, and then she babysat in the evenings and on the weekends. Everything she did, she did for me."

Charlie couldn't imagine. Had his parents ever done anything for him? Maybe. He was probably being too harsh. After all, both of them had given up their lives because of him. Perhaps they'd felt they'd already sacrificed enough. Plus, he'd had glimpses of what he'd craved from time to time from his mother. She'd be having a good day and would take him to the park or read him a story. Those times had been far and few between, but they had occasionally happened.

"You were lucky."

"Did your mother work outside the home?"

He shook his head. "She might have been happier if she had."

"I can't imagine being happier having to leave your child."

"Do you plan to keep working after the baby is born?"

Her brow furrowed. "Of course I am. I have bills."

"I'll give you child support, Savannah. Enough that you wouldn't have to work if you didn't want to."

She shook her head. "That would make me completely dependent upon you. I'd never do that. I can take care of myself and this baby. I don't need you or anyone."

She was right. She could, and would, take care of herself and their child. Her words stung, though. Not that he didn't know she didn't need him. He did know that.

Maybe he'd always known deep down. Although he and Savannah had been perfectly in tune, he'd always known he wouldn't stay and that she'd be fine. Maybe that was why he'd felt so safe letting their relationship go on as long as he had.

"I've no doubt any judge will award you a great deal of support, Savannah."

She traced her fingertip over the rim of her water glass. "I'm not going to take you to court, Charlie. All I want from you is our baby. Nothing more."

Which was just as well, because all he had to give her beyond that was money. Although she would make do and would provide just fine for their child, there was no reason for her to struggle to do so. They'd cross that bridge closer to the time for the baby to arrive. For now, he didn't want to argue with her.

"Our baby is lucky to have you, Savannah."

Glancing down at her plate, she shrugged. "Our baby will be loved, Charlie. Always."

"Like I said, our baby is lucky to have you."

Had Charlie's parents not loved him? More and more, Savannah found herself wondering about the couple who'd brought Charlie into the world.

He was such a high-functioning person that it

was difficult to see beneath the super-successful layers to the inside she was beginning to think wasn't nearly as whole as she'd once thought.

Unable to resist, she reached across the table, took his hand in hers. "Our baby is lucky to have you too, Charlie."

He winced. "We both know that isn't true."

"Regardless of where our relationship is now, Charlie, there is no one I'd rather be the father of my child than you."

He pulled his hand free. "That's crazy. There are a lot more desirable genetics out there than my screwed-up ones."

She shrugged. "Possibly, but I stand by what I said. You are an amazing cardiologist who genuinely cares about people, a brilliant man who sees things more clearly than most, a beautiful man with a body most men would envy and most women would desire to have their way with." She could feel the heat burning her cheeks as she spoke, but she pushed on because he needed to hear the truth. "You're fun, witty, and make me laugh—or at least you used to," she clarified. "All those are traits I hope our child inherits."

"I think you have the wrong guy," he finally said, looking a little uncomfortable as he took a drink.

She shook her head. "No. Although I did miscalculate a few things about you that were pointed out a few months ago, you are still you. The past few days, staying here with you and you taking care of me, has reminded me of that. Thank you."

"For?"

"Taking care of me. I hate that you've had to, but I do appreciate that you have."

"It's my fault you needed taking care of."

"My wreck was a series of unfortunate events— the fender bender that caused the initial slowing down on the interstate, the driver behind me who was texting rather than paying attention to the road. You had nothing to do with my wreck."

"It's my fault you were on that road."

"I chose to be on that road. You didn't force me to drive to Nashville. I did that of my own free will."

"You're being too generous to me."

She laughed. "No, Charlie. I assure you, being too generous with you isn't what I've done over the past few months. Quite the opposite. I keep trying to dislike you but it just won't happen, no matter how much I want it to."

He winced again. "You would be better off if you hated me."

She took a deep breath. "I thought so, but I was wrong."

"How so?"

"Because you're basically a good guy. Just because you didn't want the same things from our relationship that I did doesn't make you less of a good guy. It just makes you not the guy for me."

The skin pulled tight over his cheeks and he took another drink. "You'll find the right guy. You're a wonderful woman and any man would be lucky to have you in his life."

"You're probably right," she agreed, studying the man across the table from her and wondering if she already had found the right guy for her. "But if I never do, I'll be just fine. I don't need a man to make me feel complete. I had a good life before you and I'll have a good life after you."

As she said the words out loud, she knew they were true. Not that her life was the one she'd envisioned, but she would have a good life. She wasn't so sure about the man sitting across from her.

"I hope you have a good life too, Charlie."

He frowned. "I do."

Savannah didn't believe him.

"Truce for the baby's sake?" she offered.

He nodded. "Just so long as you understand that

for me nothing has changed from how I felt on the night I told you I was moving to Nashville."

"Just so long as you understand that for me everything has changed from how I felt before the night you told me you were moving to Nashville," she countered.

"Fair enough."

The waiter set down a strawberry shortcake with homemade cream sauce, whipped topping, and two spoons.

Savannah sighed in appreciation. "That looks amazing. I'm pretty sure both spoons are for me since I am eating for two," she teased, committed to the truce between them. A truce was the best thing for their baby, the best thing for both of them.

Being angry with him for being a jerk would be easier in many ways, but the reality was she couldn't stay angry at a man who was taking such great care of her when he didn't have to, other than the little fact that he hadn't loved her nor wanted to stick around for the rest of her life. Now that she didn't want him to, maybe they really could forge some type of truce that would allow them to raise their baby in peace.

CHAPTER TWELVE

"RUMMY!" SAVANNAH BURST out laughing and slapped the card Charlie had just played.

He glanced at the card, at the ones she'd already played, then rolled his eyes. "Obviously, I'm not paying close enough attention."

"Obviously not," she agreed, turning the cards over to show they were "dead". "It's not like you to make a mistake like that when it's just the two of us playing."

Savannah was right. It wasn't like him to make such a simple mistake during a card game, but his brain wasn't on the game.

It was on the woman sitting across the table from him. They were both sitting on the floor on opposite sides of the coffee table that had been cleared for their game.

Much as most nights over the past couple of weeks, they went to eat, then came home and played games. Cards, chess, checkers, it didn't matter just so long as they were busy.

If he didn't suggest something, she did.

It was as if they were afraid to have time alone that wasn't crammed full of something to do.

As if they might get into trouble with idle time on their hands.

Charlie might.

Although, if one looked closely, her bruises could still be spotted, overall the past three plus weeks had faded all but the larger ones. Her lacerations had healed nicely and even the sutured area on her face was looking good and barely noticeable at her hairline. Her lip was healed. Her leg stronger to where standing no longer hurt. No doubt, when she went to her appointment on Monday, Dr. Kimble would release her to return to Chattanooga. She was doing great, was over five months pregnant. There was no reason for her to stay in Nashville.

Except he didn't want her to leave.

The thought of his apartment without her left him cold.

And distracted.

"Charlie, you just played the wrong card again," Savannah pointed out when he dropped a card onto the one she'd just played. "Your head is not in this game. Are you okay?"

"Fine," he assured her, but wasn't positive that he was telling the truth.

Savannah would be going home in a couple of days.

He lifted his gaze and collided with her blue one.

She searched his as if seeking the secrets to his very being. No one knew his secrets. Some things were better kept locked away.

"Please tell me what you're thinking," she said, her gaze remaining locked with his.

"It doesn't matter."

"Why do I get the feeling it matters a great deal?"

"I was thinking about how much I'm going to miss you when you go home on Monday."

"Am I going home on Monday? Dr. Kimble didn't say that at my follow-up, just that we'd take it week by week, and I wasn't ready at my last office visit."

"We both know you're a lot stronger than you were at that appointment and the one before. The ultrasound showed everything looked great with the baby and you've not had any contractions since you were in the hospital."

"That's a good thing, though, right?"

"Yes," he agreed. "I want you well, the baby well."

"The baby is doing well." She laid her hand

across her belly that seemed to be expanding daily. Considering she'd had very little of a belly a month ago, now she had a definitely pregnant-appearing one.

Her hand moved as her belly fluttered and she smiled. "I don't know if I will ever get used to that."

He watched her from across the table as she stared at her belly and laughed out loud after a moment. She glanced up at him and smiled. "Do you want to feel?"

Did he? She'd put his hand on her belly once before but the baby hadn't moved, not to where he could feel anything other than the warmth of Savannah through her shirt.

Which was enough to have him scooting the table out to where he could get close to her. When he was settled next to her, she took his hand and placed it over her stomach where hers had been previously.

"I never know how quickly he or she will move. Sometimes it's almost constant and sometimes he or she just stops the moment I start trying to let someone else feel."

"Who else have you let touch your belly?"

"Don't sound so jealous because we both know

you're not, that I've been right here for over three weeks. It's not as if I've had an opportunity to hang out with other men and ask them to palm my belly."

"I know that." He did and yet her words did strike him with jealousy. Before he could say anything more, a little nudge bumped against his hand. Eyes wide, he glanced up at her. "That is amazing."

She nodded. "I think so every time I feel him or her move. I can't believe we'll soon get to hold our baby."

He glanced up and stared at her a bit in awe. "You really do want this baby, don't you, Savannah?"

She looked at him as if he'd asked the most ridiculous question ever. "Of course I do. How could I not?"

How could she not? How did he explain how his own parents hadn't wanted him and what a negative impact he'd had on their lives?

"Not every woman wants to have children."

"Not every man wants to have children either," she countered, arms crossing and resting on top of the little shelf her stomach made.

"Some men aren't meant to be fathers." Even as he said the words he couldn't lift his hand away from the roundness of her belly, couldn't remove his palm from feeling the miracle of life growing within her.

She placed her hand over his, tracing over his fingers. "I guess that's something we should have talked about."

"One of the many things we should have talked about."

"It's funny," she mused, staring at where his hand cradled her stomach. "I thought I knew you inside out and really I didn't know you at all."

Her words, so full of hurt and a sense of betrayal, cut him. "You did, more than you think."

She shook her head. "I didn't know the important things—that you planned to leave Chattanooga, that you didn't want children, that your career was more important than anything else. I didn't know a lot of things that I should have known."

The baby moved against his hand, just a little fluttery feel—a knee? An elbow? A foot? A hand?—rolling against his palm. His gaze lifted to Savannah's in awe.

"How do you sleep with all that going on inside you?" he asked, because he wanted to know and because he couldn't respond to her comment. She was right. She should have known those things about him. There were things he'd purposely kept hidden.

She smiled softly, stroking her fingers across her belly. "Sometimes it isn't easy. I can only imagine how it's going to be these next few months, especially if he or she has the hiccups."

His brow arched. "The hiccups? How can you tell?"

"I feel them. They're these rhythmic little movements inside me. I researched it online because I kept thinking I might be too early to feel them, but apparently babies start hiccupping in the first trimester after the central nervous system forms. I probably feel them so easily because I was so small before pregnancy."

"You're still small."

"Ha, not hardly." She patted the round curve of her belly. "Next time I feel hiccups, I'll let you know so you can feel too." Her gaze met his and he'd swear he could dive off into the deep blue of her eyes and get lost forever.

"If you want," she added, suddenly looking uncertain.

He pulled her closer to him, holding her as he wrapped his arm around her and put his hand back over her stomach. "I want."

He did want. So many things that he couldn't begin to label, or even acknowledge.

Life was better that way.

Her life. His life.

Their baby's life.

He couldn't forget that.

Savannah slid behind the steering wheel of the used car she was considering purchasing. Her pulse thundered like a wildebeest stampede across the Serengeti and breathing became so difficult you'd have thought she'd been leading the herd.

"Maybe I don't want to buy a car yet," she mused, earning a frown from the salesman and a look of concern from Charlie.

"You'll be going home soon," Charlie reminded her, his gaze coming hard her way from the passenger seat. "You need transportation."

The salesman, worried he might lose a prospective customer, reiterated, "We have other models much nicer than this one."

"There's nothing wrong with this car," she said. "I'm just not sure I'm in the market for a different vehicle."

"Well, you can't go back to driving the old one,"

Charlie reminded her as he motioned the salesman off and closed the passenger car door.

He was right. The insurance company had declared her old car totaled and cut her a check for the value. She'd bought the car used a few years ago so the amount hadn't been much. Oh, how she dreaded having a car payment. Especially now, when she'd want to take time off work for a while when the baby came along.

That was why she was hesitating.

It had nothing to do with fear.

Fear of driving.

Fear of being behind the wheel of a car.

Fear of another vehicle smashing into hers.

Fear of the pain that followed.

Yeah, fear had nothing to do with why she hesitated to start the ignition.

"Savannah?"

"Hmm?" she answered without looking at him.

"It's going to be okay."

That had her turning his way. "What?"

"I know you're scared, but it's like riding a bicycle. You'll be fine."

"I have some nasty scars on my knees from bicycle wrecks."

"But you still went right back on your bicycle every time."

He was right. She had. She'd been younger then, more foolish. Driving this car felt foolish.

"Driving the car is going to be the same," he gently told her, placing his hand on her knee. "It's a little scary just because the last time you drove you were in an accident, but it's going to be all right."

Hearing him give voice to her fears made them seem all the more real.

"You're sure?"

"There are no guarantees in life, but I do know you're a good driver, Savannah." His thumb stroked across her pants in a reassuring motion. "Statistically, that decreases the risk of you being in an accident."

"I was in an accident."

"Which statistically decreases the risk of you being in another accident."

She stared straight ahead, took a deep breath. "I feel as if I'm sitting in Driver's Education class and about to drive for the first time—only without the excited anticipation and a whole bunch of fear thrown in."

"Was that the first time you drove? In Driver's Education class?"

She nodded and took a deep breath. "Here goes."

She turned the key, started the car, and put it into reverse.

"You're pretty good for a beginner," he teased when she pulled the car out of the lot. "But if you think you're going to get an 'A' in this class, you might have to become the teacher's pet."

"Ha ha. You wish," she countered, wondering at how sweaty her palms were as she gripped the steering wheel for dear life. "So, when was the first time you drove?"

"I was fourteen and snuck out of the house to drive to a girl's house."

"Why doesn't that surprise me?"

He grinned. "She was sixteen to my fourteen. I had to do something to convince her I wasn't a kid."

"At fourteen, you were a kid."

"I didn't feel like a kid."

"Why's that?" She flicked her gaze his way, saw a flurry of emotions cross his face.

"I grew up a lot faster than some kids do."

As before, she found herself wondering at his childhood, wanting to know more.

"Tell me about your childhood."

He didn't say anything.

"Charlie, work with me here. I need distraction." She kept her tone light, teasing. "Tell me about your childhood so the fact I'm driving a car for the first time in four weeks will quit being foremost in my mind. I don't want to think about my wreck."

"I don't want you to think about your wreck."

"Then distract me."

"What do you want to know?"

"Where did you grow up?"

"Kentucky."

Kentucky. She hadn't known that.

"Your parents have both passed on?"

He didn't say anything, so she glanced his way to see the tail end of a nod. She had known that already, so she wasn't sure why she'd asked, maybe in hopes of getting him to talk about his parents.

"No siblings?"

"Nope."

"Sounds lonely."

Lonely? Yeah, Charlie's childhood could be thought of as lonely. Not that he hadn't had friends. He had. Lots of them. And girlfriends. He'd had a lot of those, too.

Such as the sixteen-year-old he'd snuck out to see the first time he'd driven a car, the first time he'd done several things. He'd been lucky he hadn't wrecked his mom's car and that his dad never found out what he'd done. He'd have beaten him black and blue.

But his father never had and his mother had decided if he was old enough to sneak out to see a girl he was old enough to run errands for her. Too bad he hadn't been the one driving the night she'd died.

"How did they die?"

Savannah's question brought him back to the present. Sort of. "My old man died of lung cancer, brought on by a lifelong cigarette habit that wasn't helped by working in a coal mine. My mother was killed in a car accident."

Savannah's foot tapped the brake harder than she should have as she stopped at a red light. "Your mother was killed in a car wreck?"

Unable to speak, he nodded.

"I'm glad you didn't lose me and the baby that way, too."

His gaze cut to her and he wasn't sure what to say. Savannah's wreck had been an accident, something beyond her control. His mother's wreck had been a single-car incident. The wreck had been ruled an accident, but Charlie had never believed that. His father hadn't either.

Not that his father had shown much remorse, or emotion at all. He'd just seemed to accept that his wife was gone.

Charlie never had.

"Me too." For a moment he allowed himself to consider having lost Savannah and the baby in the wreck. Pain shot across his chest and he immediately put the thought out of his head, reminding himself that she sat next to him, living, breathing, beautiful. He squeezed her thigh and found himself never wanting to let go. "Very glad."

What would he have done had Savannah died in that wreck? What would be different?

Everything.

She pulled away from the red light and within minutes they were back at the car lot.

"You're sure you don't want something newer, more reliable?" he asked, thinking it was his job to look out for her and the baby, to protect them as much as he could. He'd buy her a new car, one with an excellent safety record, one recommended for a single mom, with all the bells and whistles to make her life easier. But she'd already shot that down.

"I researched online and this car is rated well. It's a good price and, despite your suggestion that

I need a brand new car, I really don't need or want the expense of something new."

"I told you I'd help you," he reminded her, wishing she'd let him help her more.

She switched off the motor, turned and met his gaze. "And I told you that I didn't need your help. I got this."

"I think that's the last of my stuff." Savannah glanced around the living room as if she expected to see something she'd overlooked. "If you find something I've missed, maybe you could ship it to me?"

"Or I could bring it to you when you go into labor."

Labor. She hoped that would be at least three to four months from now, preferably the full four.

Months without seeing Charlie.

Her throat tightened and her eyes pricked with moisture. Saying goodbye hadn't been easy in Chattanooga, and it wasn't now. Maybe his having just walked away from the ultrasound had been better.

She stared at him and searched for the right words, but none seemed to really convey what she wanted to let him know.

"Thank you for taking care of me these past few weeks, Charlie."

"You're welcome." He shrugged as if it were no big deal. Possibly to him it wasn't.

She moved to him and wrapped her arms around him as much as her belly would let her.

"Thank you," she repeated, knowing she was thanking him for much more than he realized, maybe even than she'd realized until that moment. She felt a peace she hadn't felt when he'd left, a peace that came from the knowledge that, although the thought of being without him hurt, she would be just fine. She and their child would be okay, no matter what he did or didn't do.

She could do this.

He hugged her back, then tilted her chin toward him. "You're sure you're ready to go?"

She was going to miss being here with him. "It's time I go home."

He stared into her eyes, so much emotion flickering in the dark depths of his.

"Savannah." Her name came out of his mouth a bit broken and a whole lot needy.

Her lips parted. He was going to kiss her. She could feel it in the quickening of his heartbeat, in the intake of his breath, in the tensing of his body against hers, in the way he was looking at her.

The way he'd always looked at her, with need and want and desire and whatever it was he felt that she used to label love. No matter what it was called, Charlie looked at her in a way no man had ever looked at her, in a way she'd never wanted any other man to look at her, and that she doubted she ever would. This was Charlie. Her Charlie.

For the past few weeks she'd wanted him, wanted him to kiss her and touch her, and although he had touched her hand, her face, her belly, her leg, he hadn't really touched her. Not sexually. Not possessively. Not like he was looking at her at this moment.

His head lowered, his breath was warm against her mouth; her body was full of excited anticipation.

"I hope that's everything because your new car is about out of room," Chrissie said, coming back into the apartment. "Thank goodness we sent part of your stuff back with your cousin."

Savannah stepped back from Charlie just as lights went off above Chrissie's head.

"Oops, sorry. I'll be down in the car when you're

ready." She turned around and walked back out of the apartment.

Although Savannah had started driving again, she hadn't argued with Charlie when he'd told her he didn't want her making the two-hour drive by herself, especially since she'd have to cross the mountain. Her cousin had driven Chrissie up early that morning, then headed back to Chattanooga with a load of Savannah's stuff. Chrissie had helped her pack the remainder of the things she'd accumulated in Nashville into the sedan she'd bought with the insurance money plus a chunk of her savings.

She'd been so grateful for all Chrissie had done but at the moment she just wanted to scream at her friend's interruption, because somehow she knew that nothing would ever be the same once she left Nashville. Charlie would move on with his life. She'd move on with her and the baby's life. The closeness she felt with him at this moment would never again be.

Maybe it was just as well that Chrissie had interrupted.

Savannah smiled weakly at Charlie. "Timing has never been her strong suit, but I love her anyway."

"No, I imagine not." But he didn't take Savannah back into his arms, just stared down at her with so much emotion in his eyes that Savannah's heart hurt. He recognized, just as she did, that nothing would ever be the same between them, that they'd never have this moment back.

He took her hand and gave it a gentle squeeze. "Goodbye, Savannah. Don't forget to call when you go into labor."

She nodded. "I won't forget."

"You want me to help you down to the car?"

Giving him a wry smile, Savannah shook her head. "I got this."

She did. She would be just fine. She knew that. But *just fine* felt a little flat when she was looking at what could have been for the last time.

"Thanks again." With that, she said goodbye to Charlie.

CHAPTER THIRTEEN

SAVANNAH WENT BACK to work part-time the following week. Being out of work for over a month, the changes to her body during that time, had her worn out when she got home at night to where she crashed almost immediately. She worked a shift on, two shifts off to give her time to recover in between for the first few scheduled times back, possibly indefinitely until after the baby arrived. When she finished her fourth shift, she crashed onto her sofa and was so thankful she had the next two days off.

"Is my grandbaby moving?"

Savannah glanced at where her mother walked into the living room. Her mother had been a lifesaver over the past few weeks, checking on Savannah, making sure she ate. She'd brought over a plate of homemade goodies that night that Savannah had picked at before settling onto the sofa.

"He or she is always moving, Mom. You wanna feel?"

Her mother sat next to Savannah and placed her

hand over her belly. "I can't wait until I get to hold this baby."

Savannah smiled. "You're going to be a great grandma."

"I am, aren't I?" Her mother beamed, then her smile faded. "A much better grandmother than mother."

Savannah practically gawked. "What are you talking about? You were an amazing mother. I just hope I'm half as good."

"Oh, honey, hope for much more than that," her mother urged, giving Savannah's stomach a love pat. "I was such a mess after your father died. I didn't know if I was coming or going. I've often wondered if I scarred you for life."

"You were grieving Daddy. We both were a mess."

Her mother nodded. "We were and I channeled it into making sure you were everything I wasn't."

"In what way?" Savannah asked, truly baffled.

"I wanted to make sure you knew how to take care of yourself—that you never depended on a man the way I'd depended on your dad. Which in theory doesn't sound so bad, but I think I was also trying to shield you from ever feeling the pain I felt at losing your dad."

"That's not a bad thing."

"Not being able to feel that kind of pain means never loving like I loved your father."

"Pain is overrated."

Her mother shook her head. "Love is worth any amount of pain. Until you met Charlie, you never let anyone get close enough to hurt you."

"We see how that turned out." Savannah sighed. "Not so well."

Her mother shrugged. "Maybe. Maybe not."

"What's that supposed to mean?"

"Without Charlie I wouldn't be having this grandchild." Her mother rubbed her belly and the baby moved, as if recognizing the spoiling this woman was someday going to do.

"That's true," Savannah admitted. "But if not Charlie, then I would have met someone else, someone who could have loved me and our baby."

Her mother looked thoughtful for a moment. "I don't understand a lot of the ins and outs of your relationship with Charlie, but I do recognize love when I see it."

She bit the inside of her lip. "You're wrong."

"I don't know," her mother mused. "He sure went to a lot of trouble to take care of you after your wreck."

"That was guilt-driven."

"And that's your pride talking," her mother countered.

Savannah's gaze cut to her mother in shock.

"Sometimes pride can get in the way of seeing the truth."

"My pride isn't blinding me to anything."

"Except the truth," her mother said softly.

"You speak as if I was the one who pushed Charlie away by being prideful. I didn't. He left of his own free will."

"And you can't forgive him for that."

"There's nothing to forgive. He wanted to move. He moved. I'm here and want to stay here. End of story."

"Not a very good story ending."

Savannah frowned. "For someone who really hasn't said much about my breakup with Charlie, you sure are talkative tonight."

"I've been holding my tongue because I thought you two would eventually figure out what is so obvious."

"And what's that?"

"That you love each other."

Walls went up and sirens blared. "You're wrong."

"About him or you?"

"Both."

Her mother stared at her for a few minutes, then leaned over and kissed her cheek. "Just think about the things I've said. We all make mistakes, Charlie included. Maybe it's time for you to acknowledge that you made a mistake in letting him leave."

Savannah stood, hugged her mother goodbye, then sank back onto her sofa.

Her mother was wrong.

She didn't love Charlie. That was gone.

Sure she missed him and still thought he was the sexiest man alive, but love? How could you love someone who had walked away from you of his own free will?

Her shoulders lifted at the memory of the pain she'd felt that night.

You didn't love someone who had hurt you that way.

She'd not heard from Charlie. Not a peep. She'd thought he would at least text to check on her, but he hadn't.

Then again, she'd not texted him, either. She'd thought about it multiple times, such as the evening she'd come back to Chattanooga, the night before her first shift back at the hospital, that night when she'd gotten home. She'd thought about him almost non-stop, but she didn't text and she didn't call.

What would be the point? The fact that she'd stayed with him in Nashville while recuperating had changed nothing, not really, even if their truce had clouded her mind.

Had reminded her of all the reasons she'd fallen for him to begin with. Things she'd just as soon not have remembered.

Leaning back on her sofa, her feet propped up on the coffee table, she picked up her phone and stared at it.

What would he do if she texted him?

Would he answer?

Was he at home or still at work?

She'd been gone three weeks. Did he miss her? Miss eating together and playing games together and just having her in his apartment? Did he want her back?

Then again, why would he?

He'd left Chattanooga when she'd been at her best, when they'd been at their best, and he'd gone anyway.

She didn't want him back. She'd moved on the best a pregnant woman could. They'd had something good and he'd thrown it away for reasons she still didn't fully understand.

He'd nailed home the lessons her mother had taught her about not depending upon anyone other than herself. She shouldn't have. She wouldn't make that mistake again.

Tossing the phone onto the other side of the sofa, she closed her eyes.

That was when she felt the first one.

Charlie logged off his work computer and locked up his office at the hospital. He'd put in another long one. Which was just as well since he'd cut back so much during the time Savannah had been at his apartment. He'd sure not been there long enough to be asking residents to cover his patients and classes, yet he had following Savannah's wreck.

The weather was crisp and cut through his jacket, but part of him welcomed the cold, welcomed that he felt alive.

Something he hadn't felt so much over the past few weeks.

Because Savannah was gone.

He missed her like hell.

His apartment felt empty without her. His life felt empty without her. Yet she was better off without him. He had to remember—this wasn't about him. It was about Savannah and their baby. It was about making sure the past didn't repeat itself any more than it already had.

He had his dream job. He worked for a major trauma and research hospital where he got to live his dream, something his father, his mother, had never gotten to do.

Which should have him jumping over the moon.

Instead, he had to force himself to continue to put one foot in front of the other on the trek back to his apartment.

When he reached the complex, he glanced up at his window. No light.

Because no one was home.

Savannah wasn't there.

She'd gone back to her apartment, rather than the house he'd given her. The lady who cleaned the house had told him no one had been there other than herself. Hopefully, Savannah would see reason and move into the house prior to the baby's arrival. Or maybe when she went home from the hospital. He wanted her to have the house, to have the security of knowing she and the baby always had a place to call their own.

If nothing else, she could sell the house and use the money to give her and the baby a good start.

Not that he wouldn't help her with anything she needed. He would. Already, he'd talked to his lawyer to have a trust set up for the baby to ensure money was there for college. He made a great living, had invested wisely, and there was no need for Savannah and their baby to ever worry about basic needs.

Not that she would. Savannah was an independent woman, used to taking care of herself. She'd do just fine with or without his help. She didn't need him. She'd move on with her life, find someone who didn't come with his baggage, and she'd be happy.

He wanted her to be happy.

He did.

But…

Charlie mentally slapped himself. What was wrong with him? He wasn't the type to feel sorry for himself. Especially when he had what he wanted.

He had his career. He hadn't let a woman interfere with his goals. He'd kept his eyes on the prize, moved to Nashville, and achieved what he'd set out to achieve all those years ago.

"Don't let a woman hold you back from your dream, son."

Anger filled Charlie as his father's words coursed through his mind. His father was gone, no longer in his life. If only he was no longer in his head.

What would his old man say about the woman becoming the dream?

The dream that was unattainable because he couldn't take care of her, couldn't love her and let her love him.

He walked into his living room and sank onto the sofa. His gaze fell onto the deck of cards sitting on the coffee table.

She'd left them, along with a note telling him no man who was as good at cards as he was should be without a deck.

He picked them up, shuffled them back and forth.

He wasn't good at cards. He wasn't good at anything.

No, that wasn't true. He was a good cardiologist.

Savannah's words of praise replayed through his mind.

He began to slap cards down on the coffee table, one after another in neat rows.

She'd been telling him how she saw him and he

tried to look at himself through her eyes. He was a fine cardiologist who had spent a lot of time honing his craft and trying to be the best he could be, pushing himself mentally. He did care about his patients. Every single one was someone's family member, possibly some little boy's only lifeline to affection.

Savannah's other words of praise soared through his mind.

He didn't know about how enviable his body was, or even how desirable, but he did enjoy pushing himself physically, too.

Taking in the stacks of cards in front of him, he began turning over the cards remaining in his hands in sets of three.

He'd made her laugh.

Thinking back over the year they'd been together, they'd laughed a lot. More than he had his entire life. More than he'd known he could laugh.

Even this past month, once they'd called their truce, he'd laughed, and so had she.

He'd been happy.

Guilt hit him. He didn't deserve to be happy.

Not when he'd been the reason his parents had been so unhappy.

A memory of Savannah talking about their baby,

of her palm resting protectively over her rounded belly, of the joy in her voice when she spoke of their child hit him.

That was what a baby should give to his or her parents.

A baby was a blessing, wasn't that what Savannah had said?

Their baby was a blessing.

His parents hadn't seen him that way. He tried to imagine the resentment, almost hatred he'd felt emanating off his father, the apathy he'd felt from his mother at times, and he tried to imagine feeling that way about his and Savannah's baby.

He couldn't.

He tried to imagine if he'd been at a different point in his life, if he'd been in school still, or maybe not even in school yet, and how he would have felt if he'd had to change his dreams because of a baby, and tried to let the way his father had felt wash over him.

It wouldn't.

The stacks of alternating colored, numerically sequenced cards in front of him grew as he continued to slap them down.

He tried to imagine Savannah being so overcome

by life and depression and whatever else his mother had been facing that she'd take her life.

He couldn't.

Savannah was a strong woman. She would fiercely protect their child, and she'd love their child. No matter what.

She'd never dump the emotional load on their child that his parents had dumped on him.

She would be a good mother.

He'd been right when he'd told her that their child was lucky to have her.

He flipped over an ace and started a new stack as Savannah's words dug into his mind.

Their baby was lucky to have him, too.

Not really. Look at what a great start to being a dad he'd already made. Then again, wasn't being out of the picture what he believed was the best for his child? For Savannah?

He shifted through the cards, faster and faster, building the stacks in front of him, until only two cards remained.

He'd not been able to protect his mother from his father's abuse, nor had he been able to protect her from herself. His very existence had driven her to end her life.

He couldn't protect Savannah from being like

his mother and he'd rather die than drive her to that state of unhappiness, to destroy a child's self-esteem and sense of lovability, the way his parents had his.

Savannah deserved so much better.

His own parents hadn't loved him. How could he ever expect someone else to love him? To really deep down love him?

He played the last two cards and stared at the game he'd just won.

Yay for him. He'd just won at Solitaire.

Which pretty much summed up his life expectations.

His head became too heavy to hold up and he dropped his face into his hands.

He could win at being alone.

He might lose if he tried another life game. The stakes were certainly a lot higher. The possible casualties tragic.

His life goal had been a game of Solitaire.

Because he'd thought he wasn't worthy of being part of a team, not outside his career.

He and Savannah had been a team. A good one. When he'd gotten the job offer in Nashville, he'd almost said no because he hadn't wanted to leave her.

Which had scared the hell out of him and put him into defensive panic mode.

He glanced up, stared at the cards through blurry eyes.

He'd devastated Savannah, had seen the walls she'd built at his betrayal. She'd cared for him and he'd hurt her. She didn't need him and wouldn't risk letting him behind those walls again.

But he needed to be behind them.

How was he supposed to convince her to love him the way she loved their baby? That he wanted to spend the rest of his life being a team player? Being on her team and always having her back? And knowing that she'd always have his? That they'd love their baby and protect it from the harsher realities of the world together?

He scooped up the cards. Maybe he'd start with asking her to play him in a game of cards.

A game with really high stakes.

CHAPTER FOURTEEN

SAVANNAH SHOULDN'T BE doing this.

But she had made a promise.

A promise she intended to keep, no matter how difficult doing so felt. She gripped the phone as the other end of the line rang.

"Savannah?"

Charlie's voice sounded so good. Better than it should have. And worried. Very worried.

"Is everything okay?" he asked.

Squeezing the phone tighter between her suddenly clammy fingers, she cleared her throat. "I told you I'd call and so I'm calling."

"You're in labor? It's still too soon."

She shook her head, then realized that he couldn't see her. "No, I'm not in labor. The other promise I made you."

Silence came over the line, then he softly said, "Our baby has the hiccups?"

She nodded, then rolled her eyes at herself. How ridiculous that she'd called him to tell him something so trivial. He was two hours away. She'd promised to tell him so he could place his hands on her belly and feel the magic inside. He probably thought she was crazy.

"Yes," she said, feeling foolish. "The baby has the hiccups. I can feel them with my hands, so I really think you could, too."

But he didn't ask her why she was calling to tell him something so trivial, nor did he tell her she was crazy. He simply said, "I'll be right there."

She believed him. She didn't question the two-hour drive from Nashville to Chattanooga. Nor did she tell him it was doubtful the baby would still have the hiccups two hours from now. Goodness, she hoped not! Instead, she told him to be careful, which he couldn't have been because a knock sounded on her front door twenty minutes later.

When she saw Charlie on the other side of the peephole, she unlocked the door and flung it open.

"Charlie? How?" she asked, not understanding how he'd gotten there so quickly.

Looking a bit sheepish, and maybe a little uncertain as to what kind of welcome he'd receive, he reminded her, "I told you I'd be right here."

"But…how did you get here so quickly? No matter how fast you drove, you couldn't have gotten here this quick. I'm not even sure if you could have gotten here this quick by helicopter."

He shrugged. "I didn't have to drive fast to get here. I was just outside Chattanooga when you called."

She stared at him incredulously. "You were?"

He nodded.

But that meant... "Why?"

He gave a half-shrug. "I had a premonition about those hiccups. Let me in before Mrs. Henry calls the law?"

He smiled and it was the most beautiful thing she'd ever seen, making her take a step back.

He came into the apartment. She closed the door behind him, turned to look at him, not quite believing that he was really there, that he'd been on his way to Chattanooga when she'd called.

"You having any other premonitions?" she asked, not sure what to say now that he was here. She felt ridiculous for calling him, and yet he had already been on his way to Chattanooga. *Why?*

A light shining in his eyes she hadn't seen for quite some time, he grinned down at her. "A few."

"Such as?"

"That I'm going to kiss you and you're going to tell me that's okay."

Her heart grabbed hold of her ribs and rattled them around a bit. "You're sure that's your premonition?"

He nodded. "Is that okay?"

She should tell him no. She really should. But he had just driven for two hours.

"I suppose it's okay."

He kissed her. Her mouth. Her throat. Her face. He kissed her as if he were starved for her and hadn't seen her in a month of Sundays rather than just a couple of weeks ago.

He kissed her as if he'd missed her.

He kissed her until her feet floated off the ground and her insides turned to putty.

Then he kissed her more.

Dropping to his knees, he lifted the gown she wore, revealing her very round belly.

Even in the three weeks since she'd seen him, her belly had expanded. She wasn't svelte or sexy or anything that would light any fires, but she stood proudly anyway, because this was her body, their baby growing inside her.

His gaze lifted to hers and she saw the emotion there, that same one she'd seen all those months ago and thought it meant he loved her, the same one she'd questioned time and again when she'd been in Nashville. She wouldn't fool herself that love was what she saw now, but there was something. Something sweet and pure and real.

He leaned forward and kissed her belly as if it were the most precious thing ever. It was.

Her knees threatened to buckle and she grabbed hold of his shoulders to steady herself. Why was he kissing her? Why was he caressing her belly?

"I guess the hiccups are gone?"

She nodded, staring down at him with her confusion no doubt showing on her face. She couldn't have hidden it if she'd tried.

"I'll just have to stick around until the next time. Let's hope it takes a while, because I don't have any place to go and definitely don't feel up to driving back to Nashville tonight."

"You can stay here." After all, he had let her stay at his place while she recuperated. Letting him stay was the least she could do.

"That's a great idea," he said, kissing her belly again as his hands caressed her. "But we'll have to figure out some way to pass the time."

Was he suggesting…? Surely not. She'd stayed at his place for a month and he hadn't made sexual advances toward her other than when he'd kissed her. To think that within five minutes of him being back in Chattanooga he'd be propositioning her was crazy.

"Let's play cards."

"Cards?" Were her fingers digging into his shoulders? Probably, but she had to hang on because she felt off kilter.

"Yep. I have the deck you gave me in my pocket."

"Is that what that is?"

He grinned up at her. "What did you think it was?"

Still not understanding why he was there, why he was kissing her, her belly, and not understanding him wanting to play cards with her, she took a step back.

"Fine. Let's play cards, but no whining when I beat you."

He followed her to the sofa, pulled the coffee table closer. "I'm changing up the rules a little for this game."

"Sure you are. How else do you have a chance of winning?"

"Something I've realized, Savannah, is that when I'm with you, I'm always the winner."

She wrinkled her nose at him. "Have you been drinking?"

He frowned. "You know I don't drink."

"Why are you here, Charlie, because I know it's not to play cards with me?"

"You called," he reminded her.

True, she had.

"You were already on your way here."

He nodded. "I was."

"Why?"

"To ask you to play cards with me."

"You were sitting around in Nashville, bored, and decided you'd drive two hours and ask me to play a game of cards?"

He snorted. "Would you believe that's exactly how it happened?"

Rolling her eyes, she shook her head and sat down on the sofa. "Fine. We will play cards. What are we playing and what are these new rules that are supposed to help you win?"

He pulled the deck of cards from his pocket, then dragged a chair to sit opposite the coffee table from her. "You choose which game you want to play."

"Solitaire," she flung out at him.

For the first time since he'd entered her apartment, the sparkle in his eyes dimmed. "No Solitaire. You have to choose a game we can play together."

"How can you change the rules to a game if I'm the one who chooses the game?"

"You'll see. Just choose a game."

"Fine." She named a game.

"Good choice."

"So what are these new rules that are supposed to help you beat me?"

"I don't want to beat you."

"You drove two hours to lose?"

No, Charlie hadn't driven two hours to lose. Just being near her already made him feel like a winner.

"I've already told you, I'm always a winner when you and I play together."

"Right." Her tone was sarcastic and she rolled her eyes as she reached for the cards he held. "I'll deal first."

He handed her the cards, watched in silence as she dealt. When she set the cards onto the table, she glanced up at him, eyes full of expectation.

"Time for you to tell me these rules, unless you're planning to make them up as we go to increase your odds."

He took a deep breath and hoped this went the way he'd been rehearsing it in his head for the past two hours.

"The rules really haven't changed so much as the stakes."

"The stakes?"

"Winner takes all."

"All of what?" she asked as she arranged her cards in her hand.

"Whatever he or she wants from the other."

"But I don't want anything from you," she reminded him, frowning.

"Maybe you'll think of something while we're playing." Maybe he'd think of something to help him win because she sure hadn't dealt him the best hand he'd ever been given.

"Then you agree that you think I'm going to win?"

With the way his cards currently looked, probably.

"It wouldn't be the first time, but, truth is, I plan to win this game." He did. Somehow. Some way. He would win.

"Because you want something from me?"

He nodded, studying his cards so intently he hoped connections that weren't there would suddenly appear.

"What?" she asked, as if unable to help herself.

Good, he needed her to be interested. He needed her a lot more than that.

"You'll find out after I win."

"Ah, *that's* your strategy," she accused him, drawing a card from off the top of the deck. "Try to convince me to let you win. Better luck next time. I'm not that kind of girl."

The corners of his mouth tugged upwards. "I know. I like that about you."

She tossed a card from her hand down onto the table.

"Actually, there are a lot of things I like about you," he said, going for casual despite the fact his insides quaked.

She glanced at him from above the cards she held.

"Like how smart you are," he continued.

"Yes," she intoned. "All men like smart women. It's always their favorite quality in the opposite sex."

"I'm not all men, and I do admire that quality in you. Along with quite a few others." He drew a card off the top of the deck, then discarded one he didn't need.

When he didn't elaborate, she asked, "Such as?"

"Such as how intensely blue your eyes are when

curiosity is burning inside you," he teased, buying himself a little time to try to figure out how to play his cards right. Figuratively and literally.

"That's corny and superficial."

"You're a beautiful woman, Savannah. You've always turned me on."

She glanced down at her rounded belly. "Oh, yeah, I'm the stuff dreams are made of."

He nodded his agreement. "You are. My dreams."

Her mouth pinched into a tight line. "Don't say things like that."

She picked up the card he'd discarded, placed it into her hand, then tossed one she didn't want.

"Why not? It's true."

She set her cards down on the table. "If this is your strategy to win, I don't like it. Nor is it going to work."

He arched a brow. "What would work?"

"To beat me in cards?"

He nodded.

Her gaze narrowed. "Cheating?"

He shook his head. "I won't cheat you, Savannah. Not ever again."

Her mouth fell open. "You cheated me?"

"Not like what you're thinking. This was more a case of cheating myself."

"Now I'm really confused," she admitted, picking her cards back up and gesturing for him to take his turn.

He did, liking the card he drew, and tossing one of the useless ones from his hand onto the table. "I was cheating myself of what you and I could have had, because I was scared of how I feel about you. Scared of us."

There. He'd admitted the truth to her. A big truth that left him vulnerable. But it wasn't enough and he knew it.

"When I got the job offer from Vanderbilt, I felt I couldn't say no. To do so would mean admitting that you were more important to me than my career or anything else."

She took her turn, quickly drawing and discarding. "I never wanted to stand in the way of your career."

"You didn't. But the truth is my career was only an excuse to leave."

"Why did you need an excuse to leave?"

He picked up a card, tucked it in beside another card, then discarded. "Because I didn't deserve you or the happiness I'd found with you."

"Because?" she asked as she snatched up the card he'd discarded.

Part of him questioned their sanity. Here they were, having the most important conversation of their relationship, and they were playing cards while doing so. Yet wasn't that what he'd intended to some degree?

Maybe because he'd needed something to focus on besides what he was admitting to her.

"Because I destroyed my parents' lives." The admission spilled free from his lips much easier than he'd expected. Because he was telling Savannah. Because he knew he had to tell her everything before the past could be healed. God, he hoped the past could be healed. "How could I be so happy when, because of me, they'd been so miserable? I was afraid I'd do the same thing to you as I'd done to them."

It wasn't exactly fear he saw in her eyes, but the emotions glimmering there were definitely not happy stars and rainbows.

"No, afraid is too mild a word," he corrected. "I was terrified I'd do the same thing to you."

"What did you do to your parents?" Her question came out as barely more than a whisper.

He took a deep breath and spoke the truth. A truth it had taken him too many years to accept. "Exist."

Savannah's brows rose and she lowered her cards. "What?"

"You heard me."

"But I sure didn't understand you. How did existing make your parents miserable and how does that affect me?"

Here went everything on the line. He'd lay it all out there and what she did with it was up to her.

"There's a lot I haven't told you, that I haven't told anyone. My parents married because my mother was pregnant with me. They hated each other," he continued. "I'm not sure it was that way to begin with, but definitely from the time I can remember, they detested each other."

"That's sad," she said and her sincerity echoed around them.

"Very. I always wondered why they didn't divorce." He raked his hands through his hair. "I wanted them to divorce. My dad had planned to go to medical school. He had a scholarship for his undergraduate and excelled at school. When my mom got pregnant, he married her, took a job at a local coal mine, dropped down to going to school at night. He lost his scholarship when he went from full-time to part-time. Eventually, he quit going altogether. He never forgave my mother for ruining his dream, and neither of them ever forgave me for destroying everything."

"I'm sorry," she offered simply.

"Me, too. They both lived in misery. My father was determined everyone else should be at least as miserable as he was or as close as possible. He pretty much succeeded."

"That's terrible," she empathized. "I can't imagine placing that type of emotional burden on a child."

Charlie could all too well.

"My father was determined that I wouldn't make the same mistakes he'd made. I hear his voice in my head, telling me to always put my career first, to never let anyone stand in the way, and I didn't."

Savannah winced. "This is where I come in. It's okay, Charlie," she assured him. "I don't want to stand in your way. I've never wanted that. I'm fine, I promise."

Charlie took a deep breath, set his cards down and reached for Savannah's hand, and wondered if she'd ever be able to forgive someone with as messed-up a head as his. He wouldn't blame her if she couldn't.

Still, he had to tell her everything.

"It's not fine, Savannah. I'm not fine."

She frowned at him. "I don't understand."

"I've made so many mistakes over the past few months. I let you and I go on too long. When the job offer came, I didn't want to go. I took it because I felt I had to protect you."

"Protect me from what?"

"Me."

She blinked at him. "From you?"

"My father was not a good person, Savannah."

"You aren't your father," she reminded him.

"No, I'm not, but I am what drove him to that point. What drove my mother to that point. I wasn't able to protect her from him. I tried and it only made things worse. A lot worse."

"You were a child, Charlie. A blessing. It wasn't your job to protect your mother. That was your father's job."

"He's who she needed protecting from."

Understanding of just how bad things had been dawned and empathy showed in her eyes. "Did he abuse you?"

Charlie's jaw worked back and forth, memories of a fist crunching into the bones hard racking through him. "Only once."

Her brow lifted.

"I stopped him from hitting my mother. For

years, I'd blocked out what I didn't want to deal with, pretending I didn't know. One night, when I was fifteen, I couldn't pretend anymore, and I stepped in, refused to let him hit her again."

"Oh, Charlie," Savannah empathized. "Surely that had your mother waking up that she needed to get you both out of that bad situation."

"She got out," he said, trying to keep his voice steady. "She killed herself that night, but not before telling me that it was my fault he hit her and my fault she was leaving. She died because of me."

It was the first time he'd given voice to what he knew in his heart. He'd not been able to protect his mother and she'd taken her life to escape the reality of her world. A world Charlie had helped shape into the unbearable mess it had been.

Savannah gasped, then frowned. "I thought your mother died in a car wreck."

"She did."

"Oh."

Oh. Charlie's head dropped and he wondered why he was telling Savannah all this. He'd never told anyone. Maybe some things were better left unsaid.

"I'm not sure what to say."

See, Savannah agreed.

"I don't expect you to say anything."

She pulled her hand from his and rested it protectively over her belly. The motion was very telling and he struggled to continue onward with his admission.

"Caring about another person terrifies me," he admitted. "Being responsible for another person terrifies me."

"You aren't responsible for me."

"But I am responsible for our baby."

"I've not asked you for anything," she reminded him. "You don't have to be any more responsible than you want to be."

"That's just it," he admitted. "I want to be responsible in every way. For our baby and for you, Savannah. That's what the stakes are. I want you and our baby. I want you to give me a chance to make things right."

Her blue gaze lifted to his, seeking answers to the questions he saw in her eyes.

"That isn't a game, Charlie. You can't just win those things."

He closed his eyes, then opened them, stared into hers. "No, I know I can't win those things. Not really. But playing a card game with you seemed like as good a place as any to start trying to win you back into my life."

"I wasn't the one who left," she reminded him, her chin lifting a little higher.

"Words aren't my strong suit and I'm obviously failing miserably at telling you what I'm trying to say. Let me try again." He took her hand back into his, kissed her fingertips. "Savannah, you are my dream. The only one that really matters. You and our baby. I don't want to ever hurt you or make you miserable or have you look at me with anything other than happiness in your eyes. Until tonight, I never let myself consider that it wasn't me who'd made my parents miserable, but that they'd done that to themselves."

"You were an innocent child, Charlie. Of course it wasn't your fault."

"But I didn't see that, Savannah. Not until you showed me the truth. Forgive me, Savannah," he continued. "Forgive me for not seeing what was right in front of my eyes."

Tears streaming down her cheeks, she refused to look directly at him. "It's not my forgiveness you need, Charlie."

Was she unable to give him a second chance?

He'd known it was possible, but he'd hoped otherwise.

"You need to forgive yourself," she continued, her words cutting deep into his chest.

Forgive himself?

"You feel guilty that you were born, that your parents had to raise you, that you tried to protect your mother from your horrible father. Charlie, how would you feel if that was our child?"

"That's what I don't want to happen."

"It never would," she said so confidently that he stared at her in wonder. "You would never hit me, Charlie."

He grimaced at the thought of physically hurting her. He couldn't imagine any circumstance where he ever would.

"Nor would you ever mentally and emotionally abuse our child into believing he or she was to blame for your own miserable life. Your father was an ill man, Charlie. I didn't know him, but he obviously needed help."

"Probably."

"Definitely," she corrected. "As for your mother—" she let out a long breath "—I don't know why she stayed, but she was no better than he was. It was her job to protect you, Charlie—" she stressed her words "—not the other way around. She should have removed you from that situation before your dad ever had the chance to get inside your head, before you were ever put in the position of having to step in to stop her from being physically abused, and she sure shouldn't have said the things she said to you on the night she died."

He closed his eyes. "Logically, I know you're right, but how do I know I won't turn out just like them?"

"That one's easy." She took his hand and pressed a kiss to it, looked up at him with her tear-filled blue eyes. "Because you didn't."

He started to deny her claim, but stopped. She was right. He wasn't like his father. He wasn't like his mother either.

His heart surged with emotion. "I love you, you know."

Tears now spilled over onto her cheeks.

"I've never said those words out loud as an adult, not to anyone, but they're true. I love you, Savannah, and I need you in my life. Now and always. I was afraid I would do to you what my father did to my mother, what I thought I'd done to her. But I was wrong."

Leaning over to wrap her arms around him as

best she could, she buried her face against his neck. "I can't believe you're really here, that you're really saying these things to me."

"I should have been here every day, telling you how I feel every day. I don't want to lose you, Savannah. Please tell me I haven't. At least agree to play me for the chance to win a second chance. I promise not to blow it this time."

She straightened, wiped at her tears, then picked her cards up again and nodded.

"Okay?" he asked, not exactly sure what she was agreeing to.

"Let's play cards, Charlie."

He picked up his cards, looked at his still sorry hand, then nodded. He might not win this game, but he was determined to spend the rest of his life trying to win the love and respect of the woman sitting across from him.

Without another word, they each took their turn, studying their cards carefully before each move.

Finally, prior to Savannah laying down her discard, she met his gaze. "So, if you win this game, you get a second chance with me?"

He nodded.

"And if I win?"

"Did you ever figure out what it was you wanted?"

She nodded, then tossed out a card.

The card she tossed fitted perfectly into Charlie's hand. One more card and he'd be able to lie down. He wasn't sure how he'd pulled his hand together, but with each round things had improved.

"Care to share what that is?" he asked as he discarded.

"If you want to know," she said as if it were no big deal as she drew then tossed another card. A card that went perfectly with the card she'd previously tossed down.

The card Charlie needed to be able to lie down and win the game.

His gaze dropped to the discard pile, then he glanced up at her. "It's not like you to toss away cards you need."

"I don't need those cards," she denied.

"No?" He arched his brow at her. "Let me see your hand, Savannah."

She frowned. "I thought you said you wouldn't cheat."

He turned his cards up on the table, revealing them, but he didn't declare himself the winner, even though he was.

And not just at the card game.

Her gaze dropped to his cards for a brief moment, then she smiled. "You win."

"Because you cheated."

Her lips twitched.

"Let me see your cards, Savannah."

She slowly flipped her cards over. Recalling the cards she'd tossed her previous few plays, he shook his head. "Cheat."

"I didn't cheat."

"You didn't win when you should have."

"Maybe I didn't want to win at cards."

"Since when?"

"Since you changed the game rules."

His heart surged with what she meant.

"I love you, Savannah."

"I think I've always known that, Charlie. Even when you left me, deep in my heart I just couldn't accept it."

"I'm sorry I left, Savannah. I thought I was doing the right thing."

"For future reference, anything involving you leaving me is never the right thing. I love you, Charlie."

"I can't believe I'm lucky enough for you to love me."

"It's easy to love you, Charlie," she assured him. "You're a very lovable man."

Something inside him cracked at her words. He was lovable. Savannah said so and he saw the sincerity in her eyes, heard the conviction in her voice. He was lovable and she loved him.

"Thank you," he told her, kissing her face. "Thank you for that." Knowing she'd just given him a great gift that she'd probably never fully understand.

At that moment, her eyes widened, and then she smiled. Taking his hand into hers, she placed his palm against her belly. After just a couple of seconds he felt the tiniest little jolt. A few seconds later, he felt another.

He grinned. Hiccups.

They sat there in silence for a few minutes, him taking in the miracle of the life they'd created.

"I don't know how to be a good parent, Savannah. I'll need your help."

"You'll be a great daddy, Charlie. You already have the most important part down pat."

"What's that?"

"Love."

That he did, because he did love this woman and their baby with all his heart and always would.

EPILOGUE

"ONE. TWO. THREE. Blow out your candles!" Savannah told the sweet three-year-old blond-haired little boy leaning over the picnic table to get to his birthday cake.

"I can't believe my baby is three," Chrissie whined from beside the table as she removed the candles once he'd extinguished all the flames.

Savannah's mother sat near her, holding the sweetest baby girl in the whole world.

Yeah, Savannah had a difficult time believing Amelia was already three months old, too. Time sure flew when one was having fun.

She was having fun.

Mainly due to the handsome man snapping pictures to capture the moment. He caught her looking at him, grinned, then snapped a picture of her.

She rolled her eyes at him, causing him to laugh out loud, and take another photo.

After cake had been served all round, Savannah took Amelia so her mother could eat. At least that was her excuse. Really she'd just been away from her precious baby too long.

"She okay?" Charlie asked, stepping up and kissing the baby's head. Although Amelia's eyes were blue as could be, she'd gotten her dad's dark hair. Savannah knew that most babies' eyes were blue but, due to the lighter than normal shade, she suspected Amelia would keep hers. If she ended up with dark eyes like her father's that would be just fine, too.

Either way, she had both her parents wrapped around her tiny fingers.

"She's perfect," Savannah assured him and meant it in every way possible.

"You want me to hold her so you can have some birthday cake?" Charlie offered, reaching for the baby.

Savannah laughed. "That was my excuse when I took her from my mom."

He grinned and stroked his finger across Amelia's head. "You're right, you know. She is perfect."

Savannah glanced down at the wiggling little bundle in her arms, who'd realized it was past time for her next feed and her mommy now held her. Although she'd struggled for the first few days with breastfeeding, she and Amelia had eventually gotten it figured out and she was thriving.

"She takes after her daddy."

"Her mommy," he corrected, his voice choked up. Charlie glanced around the backyard of the house he'd given to Savannah but that she hadn't accepted until he'd carried her over the threshold as his wife, when he'd brought her home from the hospital after she'd delivered their daughter.

She smiled at him, knowing losing that card game to him was the best decision she'd ever made. Not that she'd let him win since. She hadn't. Not that they finished most card games they started. They usually got distracted after just the first few hands.

She'd refused to marry him until after the baby had been born. They'd gotten married at the hospital with her mother and Chrissie there, along with their daughter.

They'd traveled back and forth between Chattanooga and Nashville more than Savannah liked to consider over the past few months, but no more. Although she'd offered to move to Nashville, Charlie had refused. He'd finished his obligation to Vanderbilt last month and he was home to stay.

Home with his family.

Home where he was loved and loved her right back.

Home.

* * * * *

If you enjoyed this story, check out these other great reads from Janice Lynn

IT STARTED AT CHRISTMAS...
SIZZLING NIGHTS WITH DR OFF-LIMITS
WINTER WEDDING IN VEGAS
NEW YORK DOC TO BLUSHING BRIDE

All available now!